THE RELUCTANT TERRORIST
In Search of the Jizo

by Caleb Kavon

Proverse Hong Kong

The Reluctant Terrorist: In Search Of The Jizo is set in contemporary Hong Kong and Japan, with flashbacks to the Second World War. A Japanese businessman takes a deliberately modest revenge against another Japanese family which damaged his own during the Second World War. His surprising act of terrorism is a paradoxical gesture for peace.

We meet again characters from Kavon's first novel, *The Monkey in me: Confusion, Love and Hope under a Chinese Sky* (2009).

Caleb Kavon was raised in Hong Kong and the Philippines and has the degree of Bachelor of Arts in Third World History. He has received advanced specialized training, including in management. A former US army officer deployed in Central and South America, Kavon has lived and worked in China since 1994. He has travelled the world and remains an avid student of all things. Fluent in Chinese and Spanish, he currently lives in Chengdu, China and eagerly awaits the positive changes on our planet which he knows are possible. His first novel, *The Monkey in Me: Confusion, Love and Hope under a Chinese Sky* (Proverse Hong Kong, 2009) is dedicated "To the Chinese people, who have taught me so much and given me such kindness from my youth to the present day".

THE RELUCTANT TERRORIST

In Search of the Jizo

Caleb Kavon

Proverse Hong Kong

The Reluctant Terrorist: In Search of the Jizo
by Caleb Kavon.
Pbk published in Hong Kong by Proverse Hong Kong January 2018.
ISBN: 978-988-8491-34-6
Copyright © Proverse Hong Kong January 2018

First pub. in pbk in Hong Kong by Proverse Hong Kong, 9 March 2011.
ISBN 978-988-19320-8-2
Copyright © Proverse Hong Kong 9 March 2011.

Distribution and other enquiries to Proverse Hong Kong,
P.O. Box 259, Tung Chung Post Office,Tung Chung, Lantau Island,
New Territories, Hong Kong SAR.
E-mail: <proverse@netvigator.com>. Web: <proversepublishing.com>

The right of "Caleb Kavon" to be identified as the author of this book
has been asserted by him
in accordance with the Copyright, Designs and Patents Act 1988.

Cover design by Proverse Hong Kong and Artist Hong Kong Company.

Proverse Hong Kong

British Library Cataloguing in Publication Data (wrt first edition)

Kavon, Caleb.
  The reluctant terrorist : in search of the Jizo.
  1. Revenge--Fiction. 2. Families--Japan--Fiction.
  3. Hong Kong (China)--Fiction. 4. Japan--Fiction.
  I. Title
  813.6-dc22

ISBN-13: 9789881932082

Author's Introduction

When I look back now on the writing of *The Reluctant Terrorist*, I am not sure what I remember about it any more or about the person I was when I wrote it. Yes, I know I wrote it. I have the manuscript in a Word file somewhere on the hard drive of this old computer that I still own. These are my words. But they are words from a person in my past. What I write today is me. What I wrote a couple of years ago, it is hard to remember any more.

What I do remember of that time is that it was another of the seemingly endless challenging years of my life. The book itself was written, I think, somewhere in 2008 and finished in 2009.

My first novel, *The Monkey in Me: Confusion, Love and Hope under a Chinese Sky*, was being published at the time. I knew exactly where *The Monkey in Me* came from. I had been dying to write those words for years. My fingers struck each key with vengeance when I wrote it. It had to be said. I am still surprised it was ever published.

The Reluctant Terrorist is hard to describe because I have no idea where this book came from. I had never thought about anything like this before. The characters came alive from a place I do not know, and I remember working on it as if in a dream.

And it started with a dream. One night I saw myself standing over a small hill, looking at a scene of serene pine trees and a soft ocean vista. In my hands in front of me was a postcard of the same view that I was seeing. I slowly turned to my left and saw at a small distance a traditional wooden house with a small balcony on the second floor. An old woman was on the balcony looking at me, she had sad eyes, but a determined look, which was neither wistful nor imploring. But I thought I knew her somehow. I knew I was dreaming of a place in Japan.

That same morning I started writing *The Reluctant Terrorist*. Maybe, now that I think about it, this old lady from my dream was the person who became Naoyuki Sato's mother. Maybe it was her.

I saw her once again, along a tree-lined road, also near the sea, later, some months later, in another dream. I was walking on the dirt road with one of my loves. It seemed to be that this same old woman wanted to know my companion. I had the feeling that she approved of this one. It was as if I was Naoyuki and I was walking with Chiasa and letting Naoyuki's mother see the new couple for the first time. I don't know. It came from a dream and it all seems like one still.

Do painters see their paintings before they begin to paint? I do not paint, but I write. Do I always know what I am going to write before I write it? No, I do not. Everyday is different and what I will say I am not sure of until the letters start to appear on the screen. But I still dream, and this, and only this, am I sure of today.

Johnny Graham and Naoyuki Sato, his mother, and Chiasa are waiting for you, and they came from a dream.

Caleb Kavon
Chengdu, People's Republic of China

28 September 2010.

Dedication

To Liu Li and the Moon. You both stand by me during the long nights that make up my life. Were it not for both of you, the fog would be endless all of the time.

The Reluctant Terrorist: In Search of the Jizo

Table of Contents

Character List

Philip Barnes	Official at the Consulate-General of the United States of America in Hong Kong
"Big Rabbit"	Hong Kong triad boss
Colonel Chan	Officer of the People's Liberation Army
Alex Chang	Senior Bomb Disposal Officer, Hong Kong Police.
Johnny Graham	Inspector, Hong Kong Police
Chiasa Honda	Naoyuki Sato's love
Eddie Lo	Probationary Inspector, Hong Kong Police. Investigative Assistant to Johnny Graham
Naoyuki Sato	The "reluctant terrorist" of the title
Tetsu Sato	Father of Naoyuki
Mr Tanaka	Official at the Japanese Consulate-General in Hong Kong
Daisuke Tsuruyama	Father of Ichiru. Past friend of Tetsu Sato
Hiroshi Tsuruyama	Son of Ichiru Tsuruyama. Joint-owner of Matsushima Bay Restaurant
Ichiru Tsuruyama	Son of Daisuke Tsuruyama. Father of Hiroshi Tsuruyama. Joint-owner of Matsushima Bay Restaurant
John Wales	Official at the British Consulate-General in Hong Kong
Jason Wong	Chief Inspector, Hong Kong Police
Major Wu	Officer of the People's Liberation Army
Martin Yip	Business associate in Hong Kong of Naoyuki Sato Cambodian lion-tamer Mother of Naoyuki Sato

The Act and Time

9.19pm
    How he hated time, especially now.
    He checked his cell-phone again.
9.20pm
    Time was an enemy. Time was a prison. A place to go that had no substance. Why do we check time with such purpose? What was it?
    From the moment we open our eyes for the first time, we're on the clock. Time is our lord.
    Time to eat and time to sleep.
    Time to wake up and do this. Time to be here. Time to catch the train. How long did that last? What date is today? What day of the week is this? What time is that on? What grade are you in? How old are you? When is your birthday? How many years ago did this happen? When did your grandfather die?
    Your Social Security number, credit card number, date of birth, time of the flight, time to go home, time to be born, time to die.
    Can you get time back? Are we not petty?
    That was the best time of my life! I wished it would never end. That was the most miserable period of my life! How I hated the time I spent with her! I would never spend my time like that again!
    We sometimes look at time like it was a bank account. We always have time to do this and finish that. Or we have time to take your time. Run to the ATM machine and get more time. See if you can.
    Good times and bad times. What does that mean?
    Time is not a substance. It is not like air or oxygen that we can record and measure. Everyone can feel the soil of the earth. Can we feel time? My time is always different from your time. How I perceive the last ten minutes is not the same as

how you perceive it. He's driving, I'm sitting during the same moment. My last hour went slowly–you didn't notice. Time flies. We have time on our hands. We rush without time to work in the morning and gently pass the very same time on our vacations.

Do we share the same time? Are we in the same place? Does time even exist?

What was it about time? What makes it so very, very interesting? When did we really start needing to know? When did we all start wearing watches and put ourselves on this never-ending nonsensical clock?

Is Time nothing more than the twenty-four hours that the Earth passes in one rotation? Why not the rotation of Mars or sweet Venus? Or why not measure the rotation of the sun? Is the useless measurement of this and all that we have made of it really worth anything at all?

So maybe all we had was night and day, which were followed by night and day. And maybe we never had anything more than that. Maybe time was nothing more than a foolish pursuit and container of emptiness. Maybe chasing the wind was a more concrete action than chasing after time.

He thought for a moment. Maybe time was just so we could put on jewellery – the watch. It was just jewellery.

Did any of this have any logic at all? Or were we just punishing ourselves for nothing?

Time was a prison, especially now. What time was it?

9.23pm

He looked again.

9.23pm

Though he had passed sixty years of 9.23pms – every day had one – this time it was positively eating him alive. What about all the others? Where were we at 9.23pm last year on the 18th of March?

Hell, who knows? Do you?

As he thought this, he looked at the waitress in the small café where he was sitting. She was playing with her hair. Did she know what time it was? Her concept of time was probably the time she would get off work later. 9.23am last year on the 18th of March, where was she?

He was just dying to ask her. But no, that would draw attention. Better leave her alone.

9.28pm

He got up and went to the front of the coffee-shop and paid the bill. The waitress didn't even look at him as she gave him the change.

With that he was on the busy street and turned left and slowly walked a few buildings down the road.

9.29pm

So here it was. The time of his life. 9.30pm would be here soon. Sixty years of 9.30pms and this was the one he had waited for all his life. This was going to be it. He kept walking in the general direction of a bus-stop.

9.30pm

There it was. Three blocks away. A very large explosion. He could hear it. Short and sweet. Loud and strong. Breaking glass was heard.

9.30pm

The bus-stop only had three people. The bus pulled up with a soft gasp of the brakes and the clap of opening doors. He got on. It was time to go and catch his plane. It was over.

On the way to the airport, he knew that he had made a mistake. He was going to miss Chiasa, his love. He finally understood their love, and also knew how much she would miss him.

But the demons had to be pushed back. If there was any lesson he had learned in his life, it was this. He had to support the Jizo in this eternal struggle at the cost of his life.

Anyway, it was too late now.

And the tigers were being tamed.

Saturday Night: Part One

9.45pm

In another part of the city, Inspector Johnny Graham was sitting on his couch nursing a vile hangover. His couch was acting as his bed and a pillow helped him nurse a sad headache.

The soccer game was just coming on. He was not watching. Tonight he was only going to concentrate on the advertisements. They would be repeated all night. The game story would change. But he would just watch the advertisements and just for the hell of it all. Damn it all.

Then the phone began to vibrate. He let it vibrate to death. And it stopped. What a pleasure. He was not on call and didn't feel like speaking to anyone. He had nothing to do and nowhere to go.

He never thought of anything any more when he was at home. When he was off work, he was off work. When he was drunk, he was drunk. When he was at home, he was at home. Etc. Etc.

9.47pm

Then the phone began to vibrate again. He let it vibrate to death.

He was going to piss this off. He had no friends any more and no-one ever called. He didn't give his phone number to anyone and no-one ever called. He was happy this way.

9.48pm

Then the phone began to vibrate again. He let it vibrate to death.

9.49pm

The phone was vibrating again. Fortunately he was watching a Nokia advertisement. He let it vibrate to death.

9.50pm.

The phone was vibrating again.

Oh shit, he thought. Someone is really calling me. He picked up the phone and looked. Chief Inspector Wong was the name on the screen.

What a nasty moment! What did the Chief Inspector want at this time of night on his day off? Never think of work at home only think of home at home and work at work.

He let it vibrate to death.

9.51pm

The phone was vibrating. He answered it with a very great reluctance.

He heard the voice of the Chief Inspector. "Graham, where are you?"

"Chief Inspector, I'm at home on my day off."

"We need you down in Causeway Bay now. A bomb attack."

"A bomb attack? We've never had a bomb attack. The last bomb that went off here in Hong Kong was in the fireworks for the New Year's Day show. Are you sure?"

"Yes, Graham, of course I'm sure. Get over here now! This looks like terrorism. – Now! – That's an order. I'm next to the Century Hotel. Get over here now! There are injuries. Now!"

"Right away, Sir! Does that mean I'm off the egg-smuggling case?"

"Now, Graham! Get over here!"

"Right away, Sir!"

Terrorism in Hong Kong was impossible. Just didn't make sense. Suicide, that made sense. But not terrorism. He pushed his pistol into his waist-holster and headed to his car, three floors down.

Time to get into professional mode and study the incredible randomness of the world.

Flight

10.35pm
    Checking in.
    "Mr Sato. Do you want an aisle seat or a window seat?"
    "Please, a window seat. How long is the flight?"
    "Not sure. Maybe two hours. Yes. It arrives in one hour and forty-five minutes.
    "Here is your ticket. Please hurry. They'll begin boarding in twenty-five minutes. Thank you. The security check-point is over there."
    "Yes, I know. Thank you."
    So far, so good. He didn't need to look at his ticket. He didn't need to check his watch any more. The flight was boarding already. He was on the plane and out of there. He was not nervous. It was all over now. Just the last moments to go. He would never have to find his way again. Soon and very soon.
    As he got on the plane, he knew this was the final trip of his life. He turned his head to bow to the north and world he was leaving behind. He tried not to think of his loved ones. They were gone. The letters would explain it all to them and others. He hoped they could somehow fathom his reasons. He hoped there would be some good memories left for them in this world. He thought of the trees and flowers and mountains and silent seas of Matsushima Bay, and those last special moments of love and calm contemplation with Chiasa in what would soon be the ashes of just another life.
    Maybe he could see the moon from his window seat, as he took the last flight of his life. His great friend would surely see him off on this final journey?

Saturday Night: Part Two

Johnny Graham was nearly speechless. The road was blocked by ambulances. There were rows of ambulances and police vehicles. He saw a very small fire in front of a small Japanese Restaurant. He had not seen this kind of thing since his time in Beirut. Hong Kong ablaze. This was just damn impossible. In over twenty-five years on the force he had never seen this. Chief Wong was right. This was a mess. It was time to quit screwing around. His first adrenaline rush in years. He parked his car on the side of the road and ran towards the scene.

"Over here, Graham!"

It was Chief Inspector Wong, looking very concerned and a bit lost in his dinner jacket and stately grey hair. They had worked together for over two decades and never been friends. There was however a mutual respect that was earned. The Hong Kong Police Force is considered the finest in Asia. Johnny Graham had been sent to over six terrorism courses over the past ten years in case this would ever happen.

"What happened, Sir?'

"Looks like a small bomb. About twenty people have injuries. They don't look serious. The Restaurant was damaged. You're the terrorism expert. This is now your crime scene and I need this solved. Get to work, Graham. Eddie Lo will be your assistant. The Bomb Disposal team is on scene and the wounded are almost all evacuated. I'm very unhappy with your late arrival. Get on this now!

"Where is Lo? I'm glad you've put him on the case."

"He's over there by the hotel. I need a report on this in the morning."

"Sir, I'll need an entire task force on this now. When can I have the people?"

"You know the procedures, Graham. We'll decide everything tomorrow. Get to work! It's now 10.45pm. You're in charge. God help you if you mess this one up, Graham!"

15

With that, the Chief Inspector walked into his waiting Mercedes and sped away. Johnny Graham was in charge. Probationary Inspector Lo walked over.

Probationary Inspector Eddie Lo was the future. He was all you could be. Tall, handsome and intelligent. Johnny Graham was glad to be working with him again. The Chief was always smart when it came to putting teams together. Eddie Lo was the best of the best.

"Inspector Graham, I'm at your service. What can I do?"

"Get the scene sealed off right away and get the Press backed up. No statements to the Press until tomorrow morning. Tell them we're investigating and that it could be a bomb. Nothing else. I need the officers on the scene to locate and question any witnesses and I need a door-to-door search in the nearby area. Medical Services need to give me a full report on the wounded and the severity of the injuries. Get the Bomb Disposal people over here now. I'll use this location as the base."

"Right away, Inspector!"

Johnny Graham could now see the scene more clearly. A destroyed restaurant entrance. The fire was now out. The immense crowd of spectators and gawkers was being pushed back to the sidewalks by the Police. The street was being sealed off and new detachments of officers were arriving. This was going to be the biggest case of his career. As far as he knew, it was the first act of peace-time terrorism in the history of Hong Kong following the destruction of the Twin Towers in New York, which had changed the world for ever.

Alex Chang, a Senior Bomb Disposal Officer, was now walking over.

"Alex, what do we have?"

"Johnny, not sure what to say. I have my inspectors combing the area for clues. I'll have a partial report to you in the next half hour. Give me some time."

"OK, Alex. Get to it!"

Bomb scenes are like car crashes or like water slides. There is a smell and fear is everywhere. You want to laugh. You want to cry. You want to scream. You want it to end. You want to start forgetting it the minute it ends. In a morbid way, you want to do it again right after you've finished.

And given his hangover, he felt very, very morbid.

Johnny Graham could now see the blood stains on the street as lighting teams set up big LED lights on the area. Something bothered him about the whole thing. Why bomb a Japanese Restaurant? What was going on here?

Eddie Lo was back.

"Sir, Medical Services confirm fifteen injuries. Mostly burns and lacerations. The hospital is reporting some glass fragments and nails. No fatalities so far. That's good."

"Yes. This is a strange one, Eddie. What's the name of the Restaurant? I can't see the sign clearly."

"Sir, I've been told it's called the Matsushima Bay Japanese Restaurant. The owner hasn't arrived yet. The restaurant staff are trying to locate him now."

"Good, Eddie! Get him in here now if possible. I just can't figure out why someone would bomb a restaurant."

The phone was vibrating. Yes it was Chief Inspector Wong.

"What do you have, Graham?"

"Strange one, Sir. We do have a bomb. No fatal injuries. We are still interviewing any witnesses. Not sure on this one. Doesn't seem like our classic case, or Mid-Eastern type terrorism. The restaurant seems to be the target. We're locating the owner now. Bomb Disposal is getting me a report and we have units doing door to door in the whole neighborhood. We've backed off the Press. What time should I announce your press conference tomorrow?"

"Tell them 10am and that there've been no fatal injuries. We'll be announcing a terrorism task force, with you at the head, tomorrow. Good job so far. Call me later if anything critical occurs. All police units are now on alert. I'll see you at 6am in the command centre."

"Yes, Sir."

This was not going to be easy. A Japanese Restaurant?

Eddie had returned. "Sir, we're not getting anything so far. The witnesses heard the explosion and that's all. Should we keep searching? The room-to-room isn't finding anything. Everyone is where they are supposed to be."

"Eddie, that doesn't mean anything. Keep asking and searching. Get Alex over here."

"Yes, Sir. Also, the owners of the restaurant are here. Do you want to talk to them now?"

"No, Eddie. I'll interrogate them tomorrow at 11am at the Central Station. I do need a full search of the restaurant, and please seal it. They can enter, but only under supervision. Where are the owners now?"

"Sir, they are over there."

He was pointing at two men standing alone by a pharmacy. One was in his sixties and the other in his thirties. Both were very well-dressed. They looked angry and tough, not surprised, and emotionally shocked. He watched their eyes dart with hate at the Chinese around them.

"There are two guys, Eddie. There are two owners?"

"Yes, Sir, The owners are a father and a son. Messrs Tsuruyama. Both are Hong Kong residents with Japanese passports."

"OK, Eddie. Also, please contact someone in Immigration and Consular Affairs. I need information on the Tsuruyamas and someone needs to contact the Japanese Consulate-General and report this incident to them. They should be at our task force meeting tomorrow at 10.30am."

"Yes, Sir. I'll get that done and be right back."

Alex, the Senior Bomb Disposal Officer, was arriving back.

"Johnny, not much with the bomb. It looks like a simple fertiliser bomb. Some nails and glass. Not a big deal. We're doing explosive tests now. Some samples are going to the lab. The initial report will be ready in about two hours. The lab just called and two guys from the Chinese People's Army liaison are asking about this. What should we do?"

"Keep them out of there. The Chief will deal with them tomorrow. We need to analyze the data first. Thanks, Alex."

So far, nothing. And this is always the case. The last place to find the terrorist is where the crime has occurred. And this didn't look like anything special. A simple and stupid fertiliser bomb. A Japanese Restaurant and a lonely sleepless Saturday night were all he was going to get tonight.

He called Eddie to tell him that he was going to the Mobile Command Post to set up shop there.

Welcome to Cebu

Welcome to Cebu. The plane had landed. He was through customs again and was being driven to a small hotel on a side street. Here they would not ask for his passport and he could watch the news. Yes, it was there. They were reporting on a bombing in Hong Kong. Some injured. One of the first bombings since the Cultural Revolution. The Police were not saying much, but the news was that there was substantial damage to a Japanese restaurant. And that was all.

He just sat there in the room. He looked up at the off-white ceiling and rounded borders of the windows. He surveyed the desk and the wooden closet with plastic door-handles formed in a short "v" shape. He looked at the golden irregular shadow that the nearby night-lamp made on the dirty golden curtains as they jittered ever so softly with the gentle air movement of the fan in the corner of the room. He took the air in and felt his weight on the cushioned chair positioned at an angle in front of an old television. He could see the dust as it floated in the light. It was just right.

He was happy for the first time. He was part of this place. He felt like he was one with the building. From the doors, to the people in the other rooms, he was with them. He could hear the soft moaning of a couple making love in the room next door. The head-board of their bed was pushing against the wall like waves hitting the beach in a storm. When they started to argue after the sex, he could smile. Couples are like this. He thought of him and Chiasa back in Japan and the same thing had happened. Life would go on without him. This small hotel testified that life would go on when he was gone.

He was one with them, the hallways and their worn red carpeting and small lamps placed on the walls. He could see the hotel desk assistant, watching a comedy-show on a small TV in the small lobby. He could enjoy her moments of silent laughter as the comedian told a joke in a language and style only Philippinos could understand. He could see her hand on a blue pen and an open notebook. Every door, room and sink were his home and this place was perfect. The forms of the sleeping bodies on beds in other rooms transformed to his form. He was one with everyone there and everything. He would never have to ask for anything again.

The crickets were chirping outside his window on a hot night. He saw the forms of the trees, under the dim glare of a street light. Branches were curling toward the light, insects and bats flying past the trees, and he could see a few people walking into the night. He looked up and through the trees. There were the stars. There they were, finally, the stars of his destiny. The moon would be smiling for him. That he certainly knew.

He sat down at the small desk with his orange notebook to write Chiasa his final good-bye. He hoped she would understand somehow.

Yes. That was all he had to do right now. It would end soon. And he knew when. No need to check the time ever again. He could now finally wait. His destiny was there. The moon too.

Molten Metal

A few hours later Johnny Graham was finally getting some information. A lot of nothing.

It appeared the bomb had been placed in a rubbish receptacle in front of the restaurant. A fertiliser bomb with a simple timer, and made of items that could be bought anywhere. Fertiliser, nails, glass and a timer attached to a cell-phone. This was nothing. They were trying to trace the materials but it didn't look promising.

Since the bomb had been placed in a trash can, there was other débris strewn all over the street. All was being collected and placed in a holding area, to be analyzed. That report would take several days, though he could examine the débris later in the day.

The interviews were nothing. A bomb had gone off. Some people had been injured. No-one knew anything. There were no unusual people in the area.

The medical report was also good. Very, very minor injuries to about fifteen people. The bomb had been so weak that the injuries were minor. Alex was as perplexed as he himself was. Johnny had never seen anything like this. At least it was just this. Pretty miserable attempt at something he could not figure out. This would make things easier on the Government and easier on the Chief Inspector. But he would still have to investigate it to the very end.

As the task force was entering for more briefings, the People's Liberation Army guys were still waiting. They didn't speak English; but were still trying to get any information they could, which wasn't much. No-one was talking to them. That put a smile on Johnny Graham's face. His staff was so loyal and professional. He would have to talk to them but not for hours and only after the Chief Inspector had brought them in.

So what did he have?

Nothing more than a damaged restaurant, sullen owners and a few minor injuries, no worse than the acid attack in Mongkok several months earlier. But it was a crime and a serious one with a sentence of life imprisonment according to the new Hong Kong security law. He would have to uphold the honour of the Hong Kong Police on this one. The Chief Inspector would expect no less.

"Sir, the Chief Inspector wants to see you."

It was Eddie, looking as fresh as a rose and smiling as always.

And there he was. Chief Inspector Jason Wong, waiting in his office.

"Well, Graham. Not much damage. We should be OK on this?

"Yes. Not sure what to think. I'm not sure if we have a domestic case yet. A child could make this bomb. It could be nothing or something."

"Graham, the Executive is very worried about this. As you know it is very bad for our image, just like the acid attack and smuggling. I need a full investigation. We owe this to Hong Kong. Do you have any ideas?"

"Not yet, Chief. I need to look at the blast débris. Please try to keep these Chinese guys out of this."

"No problem on that. Carry on. We won't let anyone in until later today. Remember I helped you on the drunk driving charge. I need your help on this too."

"Sir, you know you have my support always. Thank you."

Yes, that was the Chief. Everything anyone could want in a manager. He would always be on top. He was god. Perfect in every way; all that the head of the Hong Kong Police should be. When others fell, he rose.

Eddie came in to tell him that the Japanese Consular official was out in the waiting area with the Chinese. That was a good one. To see the two big muscular Chinese officers sitting next to the slim definitely not sumo-wrestler type probably

Japanese Intelligence officer, was a good laugh. They were eyeing each other with various degrees of hate and Eddie was smiling at the comedy of the scene. Since no-one had been killed, the levity could be appreciated in what was going to be an interesting morning. Johnny Graham knew that sooner or later both the British and Americans would be in to find out what had happened. The British first and the Americans an hour later.

"Eddie, tell them we have nothing yet. They can come back in the afternoon after we get the Chief's approval."

"Great, Sir. I'll tell them."

The Japanese angle was disturbing. Japanese in Hong Kong and Asia had done all they could to blend into the woodwork over the past sixty years since the Great Pacific War. China, Hong Kong and Korea were especially sensitive to the past. But from Seoul to Rabaul, the war was still remembered. As a native born Hong Konger, Johnny Graham had relatives including his grandfather who had been interned from shortly after Christmas 1941 to the end of the war.

In fact at the end of the war, Hong Kong was still occupied by the Japanese. The population had dropped by considerably over one half and starvation was rampant. Hong Kong and China had suffered greatly at the hands of the Japanese. Try as they might it was almost impossible for the Chinese to forget this. The Japanese occupation had been so brutal and so violating. The Chinese could never forget, and to this day it was a bone of contention that had never been resolved in their hearts. It didn't help that the Japanese Prime Minister was always going to the Yasakuni Shrine in Tokyo, where the Japanese war dead were honoured as deities.

He hoped in his heart that this didn't have any connection to Japan, but something was telling him otherwise. Why was the Japanese consular officer so determined to get here so quickly? Why were the Chinese officers so insistent? Something was wrong here.

The Press was on the case. But not at fever pitch. Eddie had done a great job and everyone was just going with the flow. All the injured had left the hospital. That was the greatest blessing.

By 9.30am most of the blast débris had been removed and placed in a holding floor for inspection. Alex was waiting for him.

"Not much here. A lot of trash. I found this postcard from Japan and one business card. No finger-prints.

Johnny Graham looked first at the postcard. It was an oceanside picture with Pine Tree Islands seen at an angle. There were some buildings on the side of a mountain. The back said "Matsushima Bay, Miyagi Prefecture". Written in the card were the letters "HTK".

The business card was of a freight-forwarder, Mr Martin Yip. His office was in Causeway Bay.

"OK, Eddie. Get this Martin Yip in here later today. I want a search of his home and office and vehicle right away. I also want a list of all Japanese who left Hong Kong by any means last night after 9.30pm. And I need you to have the team analyze all surveillance cameras in the area, with a special look at anyone carrying packages or backpacks or things like that. Let me know on this as soon as you can."

Eddie looked at him and then at the Japanese consular official.

"Yes, Sir. As fast as I can."

The Chief Inspector came into the room. "Graham, any update on the situation?"

"Sir, nothing much. I have a postcard from Japan and a business card. The special unit will check out the business card and the postcard I'll check later."

"OK. I'm going to keep this an all Chinese press conference. I hope you don't mind."

"No problem, Boss. I'll see you at 10.30 for our first meeting."

Johnny Graham was relieved not to be going to the press conference. The Chief was right. Hong Kong was now Chinese and he was just an old relic of the past. The Chief respected him enough to tell him. And yes, he was on the hook for this. Good plan, Chief. You make the calls and I get the rap. Brilliant, just bloody brilliant.

Anyway, he needed to work on the postcard.

Apparently the press conference went fine. The Chief came in again smiling.

"That went well, Johnny. I need you to talk to the Chinese and the Japanese guy first. The Americans are here, this time before the British. You can push them back. Try to be polite. They're all just trying to help. Remember to speak Mandarin to the Chinese. They don't understand Cantonese or English. And – oh yes – I wanted to ask, why did you request the list of all Japanese, who left Hong Kong yesterday?"

"Just a hunch, Chief. Nothing confirmed yet. Not sure at all about this. It's way too early. Remember the Americans have been fighting Al Qaeda for almost ten years now and yesterday a fourteen-year-old killed five Marines in Kabul. This does take some time."

"Yes. Yes. You're quite right."

So he had to talk to the Chinese. They entered the conference room, leather shoes clapping the tile floor as in a military march, and the Chief left smiling.

"Sorry for the delay. I'm Inspector Graham."

"We're from the People's Liberation Army liaison office. I'm Colonel Chan and this is Major Wu."

"You arrived so early. Sorry for the delay. Very sorry."

"No problem. No need to be polite. We are all part of China now. Even the Hong Kong Police."

"Yes. We are. We have been working here for a hundred and fifty years now. My father was an Inspector and his father also. Where are you from, Colonel?"

"I am from Gansu and Major Wu is from Hebei."

"Welcome to my Hong Kong, then, Colonel. I hope you like the weather."

"I love all of our weather in China, Inspector; and I recommend you do the same."

"Oh, I love China, Colonel. Definitely I love China. Especially the weather and earthquakes."

"Good.... Why was there a Japanese waiting out there today?"

"Well, Colonel, this minor bombing apparently targeted a Japanese Restaurant; The Matsushima Bay Restaurant. The owners are Japanese, so we contacted the Consulate-General. This is routine. You would do the same in Beijing?"

"Not important what we do in Beijing. Beijing is Beijing. Do you have any suspects? We heard you've searched a home and office in Causeway Bay."

"Your sources are correct. We are searching, based on some evidence, but frankly I have nothing at this time. It takes time. You know that. As I have heard, you were recently in Tibet."

"Your sources are correct also, Inspector. Things take time. As you are a fellow Chinese and our fifty-seventh national minority member, I expect you to keep us informed."

"I thought, Colonel, there were fifty-six national minorities."

"Well – with you white Hong Kong foreigners – we now have fifty-seven national minorities. It's true you have a hundred and fifty years in Hong Kong, but we have five thousand years here. We expect to hear from you soon. Here is my card."

"Thank you, Colonel."

Major Wu had been taking notes. He looked up and smiled. "You know, Inspector, we're watching this very closely. Small or not small. Please also note 'Matsushima Bay' is also the name of a battleship used in the Japanese imperialist conquest of Taiwan. We do not like that place or that name. Please keep that in mind." He spoke in perfect American English.

"Your English is impressive, Major Wu. I expect you will soon know Cantonese equally well. And Colonel, I do know Major Wu is not from Hebei. He's from Sichuan. I can hear a Sichuan Accent from a hundred kilometres."

Major Wu smiled. Colonel Chan smiled.

"Yes. The Sichuan accent is very distinctive. You really are a Chinese now, Inspector. Have a good day."

They smiled again and left.

Johnny Graham was getting tired. He asked Eddie to bring in the Japanese consular official. He came in like a soft butterfly, making not a sound and with the smallest and yet perceptible shake in his right hand as he bowed and looked up at the Inspector.

"Welcome, Mr Tanaka. Sorry to have kept you waiting. I hope you enjoyed your time with the Chinese officials. You seemed to be getting along just fine."

"Not a problem, Graham San."

"We at the Consulate-General, on behalf of the Japanese Government, thank you for your prompt action yesterday. We are of course concerned for our citizens wherever they might be. We are all working to avoid terrorism and applaud your low crime rate. Do you have any information?"

"Not yet, Mr Tanaka. We are following all leads."

"So you have no information yet?"

"Nothing particular yet. I still need to talk to the owners of the Restaurant. – The Tsuruyamas, a father and son. – I will see them later. Tell me about Matsushima Bay in Japan. That was the name of the restaurant. Anything special about the food?

"Well, Matsushima Bay is probably our third most famous tourist destination. It's a scenic place dotted with over two hundred and sixty beautiful pine-covered small islands. That is the 'Shima' in the name. – It means, 'Islands'. 'Matsu' is 'Pine'. So we call it 'Matsushima'. It is north of Tokyo about four hours by train. We like to enjoy it during the summer for weekends."

"Well, I heard it was also the name of an imperial Japanese battleship in the war on Taiwan and maybe against China in the Russian Japanese War."

Mr Tanaka's eyes got very wide and he quickly said.

"I need to check on that. Please do let me know if you if find anything. Thanks so much for your time."

"Sorry for the delay. We have been so busy. I still have much to do."

"Thank you and thank you again, Inspector."

"All the best. We will be talking to you soon, I hope."

Well, this was all par for the course. The Chinese knew something and so did the Japanese. As usual dear old Hong Kong was in the middle. Johnny Graham only hoped that this time the right side would win ... whichever that was.

Next in the office was Philip Barnes, from the United States Consulate-General. Barnes was a nondescript, thin, balding American in a Brooks Brothers suit and a baby-blue striped tie; definitely not an intimidating profile for a man representing the world's only remaining superpower. He had been posted to Hong Kong only about a year ago, and was having a hard time finding his way.

Barnes was a problem. He thought anything that happened had to be Islamic in nature. He didn't know anything else. He could only speak Arabic and was here just to track Islamic problems. As a result, he was always asking for help with this surveillance on an Arab or this case on a Pakistani. He never seemed to understand that Hong Kong was an open city with constant transit for business to Hong Kong and into China. In such a place of interchange, who knows who is who, as 3.8 million people transit the international airport every month.

"Well, Johnny, I thought you said there was no terrorism in Hong Kong. Wrong this time?"

"Not yet, Phil. Need to get the facts. Sorry we didn't turn up any mujahedeen last night in our area sweeps for you."

"Well, you never know. That's why we're here. Let me know if there is ever anything of interest to us. I know you will."

"Yes, Phil, you know I will. Thanks for waiting. I'll get back to you. Have a good day winning the war on terrorism!"

"It's your war too, Johnny. Remember that some time."

"We will. Remember my great-grandfather's brother served in Afghanistan, before you Americans even got to Arizona. I understand more than you know. Were the shoes the Arab threw at the President size 10 or 12? I really can't remember."

"I know you do understand, Johnny. That's why I'm sure you will let me know what is going on here. We have never gone out for a drink. Let me know when we can meet up. I hear Lan Kwai Fong is very happening now."

"OK, Phil. Thanks. Let me get back to work."

Next was the British Consulate-General staffer, John Wales. He was your prim and proper MI # whatever type. Unlike Johnny Graham, he wasn't from Hong Kong and he was just moving his way up until the Conservatives got back into power, if they ever did. His Saville Row suit was soaked in sweat and the grey hairs were beginning to show through his styled hair cut, which reminded Johnny Graham of the new Mayor of London's hair style.

"Welcome back to your Colony, John!" he greeted him. "How's life at the club? Must be terrible to be out on these dirty streets after such an impressive round of golf."

"Thanks, Graham. You were English at some time, I do recall."

"Well yes, I did go to King George the Fifth School here. So yes, I do keep up with the Premier League. But, you know, just to watch the commercials. And I never vote in council elections. When is that seat in Parliament you want up for election?"

"Soon. I hope very soon. ... I hear you had quite a commotion last night in Causeway Bay."

"Soon does sound good. Even the Americans beat your chaps to the scene. About our lovely interlude last night, a bit of a commotion, but a short one. Not sure what it is yet. Can I please postpone the final judgement until we get some police work done?"

"But, of course Johnny. You know we're here to assist at all times."

"Well, maybe your time would be best spent in Mumbai this week, with the Prime Minister, and guarding the Taj Mahal Hotel. This was pretty much of a non-event here. I'll let you know what we get."

"Mumbai is terrible. I'm mentally always in Tenerife. Carry on, my good fellow. Keep in touch!"

Johnny Graham just couldn't help himself. He was tired of these travelling salesmen. They were just moving up the ladder and couldn't be bothered to do good work or care about anything. Hard work had its reward. He was sure.

Of course, he had to work with all of these guys, The Chinese officer, Major Wu seemed to know something and Mr Tanaka was worried. Maybe something would turn up and he could go back home.

"Eddie you take a rest. Please come back tonight. Same for Alex. You've given me all the information now. Schedule the owners for tonight and Martin Yip for later tonight. Did anything turn up with him?"

"Not yet, but he was very agitated that his card had turned up at a crime scene. Looks like a normal trading company."

"Does he do any business with Japan, Eddie?"

"I didn't ask, Sir. I was waiting for your guidance."

"Eddie, you're the best. But never wait for my guidance. We need to hunt this one down. Never wait for guidance, it just messes you up. Go ahead and bring him up to the interview room now."

"Sir, do you need me to assist?"

"No, Eddie. Please go get some rest. Remember my Chinese is better than yours and we were here before your family came to Hong Kong from Foshan. It was Foshan wasn't it?"

"Yes Sir, Foshan. It was in 1952. Thanks again!"

"Get some rest, take your mother out to dinner. You did a great job. See you tomorrow."

In the interview room a very nervous Martin Yip was waiting. He was sweating and obviously distressed. Even more distressed when a white police officer entered the room.

"Mr Yip, good day! Sorry for the inconvenience. We have to do our job especially in a case like this. I hope you understand."

"Yes. I really have no idea how my card got there. I give a lot of cards out every day, as you can imagine. Please believe me. I have never done anything illegal in my life."

"So your firm is Tech Line Trading and you trade technology goods all over the world."

"Yes, that's correct."

"Do you do business in Japan, Mr Yip?"

"Yes of course. It's a big market."

"Have you had any foreign visitors lately?"

"Yes. I have customers in all the time, of course."

"Any from Japan?"

"Yes, this is all so strange. My customer, Mr Tomoda, was here at the beginning of the week. He left a package with me for later shipment. It's in our warehouse. Maybe this has something to do with the case?"

"Not sure, Mr Yip. Please tell me, do you ever go to the Matsushima Bay Restaurant, or know anyone who works at the Restaurant?"

"Never, I was never even near there anytime this week. I live in Shatin new town."

"What did you discuss with Mr Tomoda?"

"He's a new customer. He wanted some samples from us. I gave him a new solar-energy powered digital camera, and he left a package. He said he would tell us what to do with it later. It was a really short meeting, no more than twenty minutes. He said he had somewhere else to go and left quickly."

"Good, please go with the police officer to get the package and I'll need Mr Tomoda's name contacts and business card. Also I'll need all your customer contacts and records of business and the names of any visitors you've had recently. Where was Mr Tomoda staying?"

"Not sure, he didn't say. He's a new customer and we have not really had any business. I too thought it was strange that he left a package. But we try to get business wherever we can. That is our way in Hong Kong."

"Yes, Mr Yip, we do try."

"What else can you tell me about Mr Tomoda?"

"Well, he was about sixty years old, with balding hair. His English was excellent. You know, much better than mine. I thought that was odd, and he said he had studied many things."

"Please hurry and get this package for me. I'll be here waiting."

A nearby team member escorted a shaken Mr Yip out of the room.

"Go with him and take a bomb disposal officer with you, just in case."

Now he had something to sink his teeth into. Something was up. It almost seemed as if the card had been placed at the scene on purpose. What about the postcard and the battleship? Something was pointing somewhere. This Tomoda might be the chap. But why leave clues? Why would a Japanese bomb a Japanese restaurant in Hong Kong?

Sibuyan Sea

The Super Ferry was moving through the night underneath the moon on a calm Sibuyan sea. He had left earlier that afternoon from Cebu en route to Manila. Now he was closer, he could almost see his father's cruiser, the "Kumano", crippled and being towed by the freighter. He knew the American submarines were near and waiting for them even then. They had come close to victory but now it was all over.

He stopped and looked at the moonlit sea in the midst of large islands. He pushed his hand against the rail and saw the weak shadow of his own fingers and the soft light of the moon off the simple silver ring on his third finger.

No, that wasn't it. It wasn't here. Or maybe it couldn't have been near here that the biggest naval battle of the Pacific War was fought. Not possible.

That was in another universe, so close to his life and yet so impossibly far away. He looked back out at the sea, the grave of so many over sixty years ago. He knew it was more than a sea. It was death itself. It was defeat for all of us. Nothing else.

His thinking was marred by the sudden singing from the onboard karaoke bar. Some people were laughing. For them this was a fun trip. He was almost irritated by the laughter that was draining his melancholy and sadness away. Yes, he thought, they can laugh, and we can suffer. It's just a simple choice that we all have. We can mourn forever or we can live.

He knew the Philippino people had suffered, and were suffering even now. But they could somehow laugh it in the face. He admired them for this, their strength, and only wished he could laugh with them, something he had never been able to do from the moment of his birth.

He shook his head. He would not go with them now. It was not possible in this life and what remained of it.

He took some dried flowers from his sports-coat pocket and bowed. As he lifted his head, with two hands together, he separated them and let the flowers fall one at a time in the wind that would let them drift into the moonlit diamonds of the sea. The moon was radiant at that moment. The waves shot the light back and flowers fell toward those seconds of light. Now his mother might rest after sixty years of waiting for his father to return.

He thought of their lost lives, and the lost lives of millions. These flowers could probably do no more to break the pain than one wave can break the form of a granite cliff. But that was all he was, a wave against a granite cliff, soon to lose form and melt back into the ocean.

That was all he was…that's all he could ever be. The pain was too great for all of us. It would take millions of waves and perhaps centuries to transform the agony of our sins and shame of our defeat.

He thought again of his father and the nearly destroyed cruiser, "Kumano" being towed somewhere out there on that night in the late October of 1944. This was the closest he and his father had ever been.

So far.

The nearby laughter caused him to retreat to his cabin just as the roar of a lion scurries the zebra in the afternoon quiet of the savannah on the African plains. It was too bad. But this was not Matsushima Bay.

He went back to his cabin and turned off all the lights. Only the moon would keep him company on the small bed this night. Somehow that was more than enough.

Postcards from Kure

Finally Johnny Graham was alone. For the first time in almost a day, he could think and review the case. When you're at work, you must work.

So what did he have? A bald Japanese guy.

He called the investigators to check if any Tomoda had left town last night and checked the database. There had been no Mr Tomoda arriving or departing in the past several days. The last one had left over two weeks ago. They were checking his hotel and contacts.

He called to check if any bald guy had been seen via the nearby security cameras. The camera unit could not say for sure. There was one guy who looked like he was bald but he was wearing a baseball cap and carrying a backpack. There was no coverage of the front of the restaurant and the baseball cap guy's face was not really recognizable. He had kept his face turned away from the cameras. But we did have a possible here.

Martin Yip was clearing also. His cell-phone had been used in Shatin all day on Saturday. His witnesses and story checked out. He hoped this package had something. Somehow he knew it would.

Now to check on the Tsuruyamas. Mr Ichiru Tsuruyama, senior, was sixty-five, born in Kure Japan in 1946, about six months after the atom bombs were dropped on Japan. He came to Hong Kong as a boy in the 1950s with his father, Daisuke Tsuruyama, who had started a trading business. His passport records indicated very frequent travel to China. Some different places were recorded. He was frequently in Dalian, Fujian and Beijing, Qingdao and Shanghai.

The son was Hiroshi Tsuruyama. For some reason, he had been born in Japan and had just become a Hong Kong resident. Apparently he didn't grow up with his father. He was from Hiroshima.

The crime database had been checked and both of them had been in fights in the past, usually in karaoke bars or night clubs. From what he could remember, they looked the part. With their crew cuts and snarling faces they did look tough. Maybe they were mafia guys? Maybe this had something to do with the bomb?

One of the arrest records was telling. The Chinese constable had reported that Ichiru had used racist comments about the Chinese during his last arrest in 1995. Nothing had come of that. Ichiru denied it and was released.

So these guys were not angels. But they were still officially the victims in this.

He decided to go out to Wanchai for a little while.
He could walk. The Central Police Station was very close to where he needed to go. This trip was going to cost him a bit.
Cruising a couple of blocks and entering a nondescript building, he went up six floors and knocked on the door. His police ID was in his hand. The metal door opened and three young guys with tattoos got up quickly in fear from the eight tables of men playing cards.

"Calm down. I want to see Big Rabbit."

"Who are you?"

"Tell Big Rabbit that Little Rabbit is here to see him."

"OK...please wait here."

Less than a minute later he was escorted to a side office.

"My Little Rabbit has arrived. I thought you would, after last night. I saw you on TV. You were looking very official."

Seated behind a huge mahogany desk was a tall fat man with thick glasses and a mop of black hair which was parted in the center. He was corpulent and smiling. The kind of guy everyone likes instantly. He had always been the same.

"This one is going to cost you, Graham. I know why you're here and about whom. So, what is it going to be? I need some real cooperation now. They have been hammering us as you know. Chief Wong is real bastard. He won't let us do anything any more. And you let the Chinese families get away with anything."

Big Rabbit was a local triad boss. Before the handover to China there had been three main triads and Big Rabbit controlled one of the areas on Hong Kong side. Now even the Chinese Mainland mafia was there, which is what Big Rabbit had been referring to.

After a long career which included a trip to Stanley prison, he was an old "friend." He would help the police if they would help him. Johnny Graham tried to stay out of this kind of thing, but sometimes there was no choice.

Everyone had to work with everyone. That was the Hong Kong way. His father had known Big Rabbit's father and they had even seen each other during childhood. The father – Gold Dragon – had even gone to Johnny Graham's father's funeral.

Big Rabbit was always bigger than him. Even as children, it was obvious that Johnny would be a Hong Kong policeman and Big Rabbit would one day become a triad boss.

So it had gone on for years. Sometimes Johnny would help Big Rabbit and sometimes Big Rabbit would help Johnny. If the police really wanted someone, Big Rabbit would cooperate. If there was a huge raid coming, Johnny could repay Big Rabbit by letting him know about it in advance. This was just how it was. Johnny Graham had quite a lot of fellow feeling for them.

"OK. I owe you one. What do you have?"

"You're right. These are bad guys. The father is a jerk. He's always in China doing whatever. He's with the Japanese mafia and who knows what else. He's with the Yamaguchi, I think. We don't have much to do with them, they hate us Chinese. The kid is nasty too. The grandfather was here in Hong Kong during the war. We had contacts with them in the beginning. Then they starved us all. He was let back but had to make a good payment in the 1950s. We know them."

"What about the grandfather? What did he do during the war?"

"We're not sure. I asked old Tiger Zhou. He couldn't remember. He's too old now. Almost ninety years old. But he knew that the grandfather had gotten rich during the war. He was a naval officer. Not sure. You know that was before our time. Not much before. But, it was before we were around. Remember the good old days?"

"I sure do."

"OK, old friend. I owe you one. We are old Hong Kong boys, forever."

"I'll be calling one of these days. You still have the same cell-phone."

"No. Just call the electronics store like before. I'll call you."

"OK. Life goes on. Still trying to figure this out."

"Who knows, maybe they lost money in Burma playing cards. Who knows. These things happen."

"Not in our Hong Kong, Big Rabbit."

"Yes, us locals always do a better job than anyone else."

"Thanks. I really appreciate it."

"OK. Try to get Chief Wong to relax. I think he wants to be Chief Secretary one day."

"He's hard to talk to. Maybe you're right. I'll do what I can."

"Be calling you soon."

Yes, Big Rabbit was a good friend. So they ran card clubs and whore houses. So what? Things ran pretty well. It was the drugs which Johnny Graham didn't like. But who knows? Maybe some Police were involved in all that too. Anyway, now the case was becoming strange. He went back to meet the devil in the Tsuruyamas.

Eddie was there waiting. So was Martin Yip.

"OK, Mr Yip, Thanks for the package. Please wait outside as I check it."

"Yes Sir, when can I go home?"

"Soon I hope."

Yip left with Eddie.

Wearing plastic gloves, he opened the brown paper packaging. There was another – bright orange – paper wrapping.

He opened that as well, revealing several picture postcards.

The first picture was of a battleship. This time, Major Wu was correct. On the back of the card was printed the words, "Matsushima Bay". The next card pictured another ship, "Heavy Cruiser 'Kumano'". On the back was written, "Tetsu Sato, 25 October 1944." Below it was the date, "7 July 1944," but the date was crossed out. The next card showed two very young men in Military Uniforms. On the back was inscribed, "Daisuke and Tetsu: Eta Jima 1934." The final postcard was labeled, "Yamato Museum, Kure, Japan."

Kure, Japan. He checked again. Ichiru, the father, was from Kure. This was becoming stranger and stranger. He felt like he was being pulled back in time.

He checked Tomoda's business card. It said, "Shigio Tomoda, Santa Cruz Trading, Sendai, Japan." There were telephone numbers and even a website.

"Eddie, I need everything you can get on this Tomoda guy and this company. Now! Call our people in Japan. Don't tell Tanaka. Please note this could be a fake name. There are no immigration records on any Tomodas for the past twenty days. Check the cell-phone records and everything you can get. This could be our culprit."

"Boss, Tanaka is back. I stopped him from talking to the Tsuruyamas. They're in the interview room."

"OK, don't tell him anything. I need this information immediately. Tell Yip to go home. Keep the restaurant sealed and tell the Tsuruyamas I'll see them tomorrow. Tell Tanaka to go home. We can meet tomorrow. I need this information now. I'm going to the duty-room for some sleep. Let me know about this Tomoda."

"Yes, Sir."

He made the long walk to the duty-room bedroom on the West Side of the building. His day was ending at twenty-four hours. His instincts told him that Tomoda was the one and that this was somehow more than a normal crime. The war photos disturbed him. But he was too tired to think any more. He was asleep in a second. His last thought was that when you sleep, you sleep. That is all you do.

Life on Aoba Street

Chiasa Honda could not sleep. She had not heard from Naoyuki for over a week. He had said he had to go to the Philippines. Then he sent an email from Hong Kong last week. He didn't sound good. But he said it would be OK. She was used to his overseas trips but this one made her feel different for some reason. She didn't think he had another woman. But who knew with men?

Maybe he was still angry with her. Naoyuki had seen her talking to a young man outside her beauty shop on Aoba Road about two weeks ago. This had happened several times. Naoyuki was over twenty years older than her and was often jealous. In a way she could understand. He felt threatened by the younger men whom she knew. This had always been the case. Of course, he could never understand that she loved him, and him alone. They never talked about things like that.

Naoyuki was married with several children and lived in Tokyo. They had met when she was much younger, right after she had lost her baby. She sighed at the thought and at what she had done. The day she had placed the water baby in front of the shrine was still with her.

He was obviously very rich with a big BMW and a golden watch. After they had been together for a short while, Naoyuki had helped her finance her dream, the small beauty shop on Aoba Street in Sendai.

She smiled. She was so different before. Impulsive, angry and always out at the clubs. He was a strange influence on her. He almost never talked, but when he did it always meant something. And he always listened to her when no-one else ever did. About his family, he never said a word.

Ten years with him had been just what she needed. He gave her a life. The beauty shop had done well and she had always been able to make the payments for the bank loan. Naoyuki had taught her to be herself and allowed her to live her dream.

For her, the beauty shop was everything. It was a community. Her friends and customers became a special world. Because of him and his kindness and love, she had what she had always wanted.

Not that she knew him. She really didn't. But there was a special feeling in their relationship of ten years. The quietness of the evenings when he came on his weekend visits away from the family. The quiet walks by the nearby sea at Matsushima Bay and visits to temples or the Sendai Jazz Festival which he so enjoyed every year in September. She had grown to love him more as the years went on, without ever really knowing him.

Love is a feeling. Love is peace itself. Life with Naoyuki was that for her. Yes. It would be all right, He was always right. She could sleep now. She was sure she would hear from him tomorrow. She just knew it. He was her love. He was her life.

Maybe one day, he would not be so jealous. She hoped so.

With Admiral Kurita at Leyte Gulf

Johnny Graham woke up with a start after only fifty minutes. He had more work to do before the Tsuruyamas arrived in the morning. He almost ran back to the command centre and started searching on the internet.

The "Matsushima Bay" was a Japanese warship which fought the Chinese and Koreans and Russians. Not much was there. She had been in several battles. He didn't see anything interesting about the ship that would tie it to this case.

The "Kumano" was another story. In a website, he found a long description of the vessel that had served throughout the Pacific War. She was often in Kure, Japan for refitting. The "Kumano" survived until the end of November 1944 when she was sunk off the coast of the Zambales in the Philippines.

There was Kure again.

Chronology continued

29 March 1944:
Captain Hitomi Soichiro (former Division Officer of FUMIZUKI) assumes command of "KUMANO"

11 May 1944:
Steams from Lingga to old American Anchorage of Tawi Tawi in the Sulo Archepelago with Vice Admiral Ozawa Jisaburo's (former Commanding Officer of Haruna) Mobile Fleet.

13 May 1944:
Arrives at Tawi Tawi with Vice Admiral Kurita's Force "C" Vanguard:BatDiv 1's YAMATO and MUSAHI, BatDiv3, CarDiv 3s

CHITOSE, CHIYODA and ZUIHO, CruDiv 4's
ATAGO, TAKAO. MAYA and CHOKAI, CruDiv 7s,
"KUMANO", SUZUYA, CHIKUMA and TONE, DesRon
2's light cruiser NOSHIRO and Rear Admiral
(Vice-Admiral posthumously) Hayakawa
Mikio's (former COMMANDING OFFICER of
NAGATO) DesDiv 31s ASASHIMO, KISHINAMI,
OKINAMI and DesDiv 32s FUJINAMI, SHIMIKAZE
and HAMEKAZE.

15-17 MAY 1944:
Departs Tawi Tawi with SUZUYA for Tarakan,
Borneo to refuel. Returns to Tawi Tawi.
13 June 1944. Operation "A-GO" - The
Battle of the Philippine Sea: In Tokyo,
the CINC, Combined Fleet, Admiral Toyoda
Soemu(Former Commanding Officer of HYUGA)
sends out a signal that activates the "A-
GO" plan for defence of the Marianas.

Ozawa's Mobile Fleet departs Tawi Tawi
(less Operation Kon's BatDiv 1, CruDiv 8)
for Guimara near Panay Island,
Philippines. At 1000 LtCdr Marshall H.
Austin's USS Redfin (SS-272) sights and
reports the departing Mobile Fleet.

14 June 1944:
At Guimaras. Refuels from Oilers.

15 June 1944:
The Mobile Fleet departs Guimaras through
the Visayan Sea. At 1622, the fleet is
sighted in the San Bernardino Strait by
lookouts on LtCdr Robert Risser's USS
Flying Fish (SS-229).

17 June 1944:
Lookouts about LtCdr(later Rear-Admiral)
Herman J. Kossler's USS CAVALLA (SS-244)
sight the fleet in the Philippine Sea.
Kossler reports its movement after
surfacing later that evening.

18-19 JUNE 1944:
Ozawa splits the Mobile Fleet. Forces A
and B proceed southward. The Vanguard
Force C proceeds due east in the
Philippine Sea headed towards Saipan. The
Mobile Fleet's aircraft attack the US Task
Force 58 off Saipan but suffer
overwhelming losses at the Great Mariana's
Turkey Shoot.

20 June 1944:
At 1830 Curtiss SB2C Helldiver dive-
bombers and TBM torpedo-bombers from USS
BUNKER HILL (CVL-28) attack BatDIV 3 and
carrier CHIYODA. During the battle, air
attacks sink carrier HIYO and damage
Battleship HARUNA, carriers ZUIKAKU,
JUNYO, CHIYODA and RYUHO. Meanwhile
Kossler's CAVALLA sinks SHOKAKU and LtCdr
James Blanchard's ALBACORE (SS-218) sinks
new armored carrier TAIHO. The Mobile
Fleet retires to Okinawa.

22 June 1944:
Arrives at Nakagusuko Wan (Bay) Okinawa
for refueling destroyers, then departs.

```
24 June 1944:
The Mobile Fleet arrives at Hashirajima.

25 June 1944:
At Kure for refit. Additional 25-mm AA
installed. A Type 22 surface search radar
and a Type 13 air search radar are
installed.
```

There was Kure again. This was getting to be a real time journey into the belly of the monster.

Eddie came in.

"Sir, the cell-phone was used in Hong Kong last week. We are checking where and how. I'll get back to you soon on this. Still nothing on Tomoda or the company. It is still early in Japan."

OK. Good work, Eddie. This is moving along."

He quickly checked on Kure. Yes this was a major depot for the Imperial Navy. So there was something that connected Tomoda, or whatever his name was, and the Tsuruyamas. He was not sure what it was. He hoped he might find out soon.

Manila Bay

Naoyuki Sato arrived in Manila that morning. This was it. Really nothing to do any more. He took a taxi to the Coyoacan bus terminal and took a Victory Bus Lines bus to Santa Cruz. It was finally time to get there. Sixty years of waiting and now he could see. This was the vacation his father had never given him. Like the "Kumano". Sixty years ago, he was running to the north away from the oncoming victors. He was ready to lose, but had to make the final journey.

He looked out at the city from the window of the bus. The traffic and smoke made no impact on him. He was just an observer without any interest. What he did would have no impact on them, or their lives. They would go on. He hoped Chiasa would too. She was the only one who was going to suffer in all this, just like his mother had suffered before her. He was very ashamed of his jealousy that last time he had seen her. No reason for it at all. No reason. He was so unprepared for any relationship and there was little reason to believe he could have done any more with his life in this regard.

He was raised almost in silence. He was surprised he could even talk. The loss of his father was so omnipresent in everything. His mother was broken from that day; when the final letter arrived and the notice of his death arrived. How he was ever born under such conditions he would never know. How he had lived so long after seeing such pain he would never understand. How is it? We suffer and are broken. We suffer and then recover. We fall and then we rise. We are destroyed and come back again. Yet, we forget, some of us suffer and never come back. Some us suffer forever.

His life was determined by one instant in another land. His father had served aboard the "Kumano". His father had died with the "Kumano" in Santa Cruz harbour. Some had survived, but not Tetsu Sato. His life ended, and his mother had died even before he was born. He was born to a dead mother. She could not recover from this, and it was that pain that had marked his life from the moment of birth.

He felt this pain every day of his life. He never knew any joy. He had always been sad and reflective. His teachers had called him "the crying bear". His peers could not understand him, and he never played with them. He was saved from vicious teasing by his tall frame and the good looks of his parents.

He could study and did very well in school, but felt that he never got anything out of it. He was born with a sadness that was deep inside him. How could one live when so much was lost? He simply didn't have the capacity to recuperate from a blow that had been given even before his birth. It made for this final event.

The world would have been so much better if his parents had not been in love. But they were. He saw the letters before his father went off to war. He looked at their pictures in kimonos by the cherry blossoms in Nishi Park. He knew he was the product of something special. He was the child of a handsome and sharp officer in the Japanese Imperial Navy and a beautiful dedicated woman. His father was not just anyone. He was educated and travelled, spoke English and had seen the world. His mother was more beautiful than a goddess. They were the perfect couple and like a flame this had been destroyed. All had been destroyed. Her happiness, his reputation, and the life of an unborn child was sent to ashes as if a flame had been crushed.

It was the classic dream crushed. It was the most beautiful story mangled in one swoop. What they had ruined! He could not help but feel the loss. He knew he was not the only one. There were millions like him. Millions of crushed widows and fatherless children all over the world. Millions of children wondering and idealizing a father they could never know. Millions of mothers burdened with responsibilities that were almost impossible to bear.

Naoyuki Sato could never get over the fact that he could not rise from the womb to save his father, or that he was too small to restore his honour. He could never make up for his mother's eternal silence and her daily trips to the beach to throw flowers into the ocean, the final graveyard for her dear Tetsu. She had lived sixty years after his death and each day walked before work and after work to throw flowers to the sea. He could not believe it, every day. She never talked about all of this except that once.

He was born to live this death. It was what fate had in hand for him. He was forced to avenge them. Thank God for the lion tamer.

The bus made a sharp turn and entered the highway. Four more hours to Santa Cruz.

Definitions in Dark Green

Johnny Graham continued his research as the morning turned from black to blue and grey on a cool Hong Kong morning. Kure was a major refit and logistics base for the Japanese Imperial Navy, and very close to the Naval Academy on Eta Jima. He looked at the picture of Daisuke and Tetsu in their naval cadet uniforms, a stiff pose of white cloth mixed with determination. Bravery mixed with an uncertain destiny. Yes, it was a beautiful shot. In the background was a wrinkled tree with a few cherry blossoms hanging on a far left branch. The romance of defeat was mixing with the arrogance of past victories. Who knows what had happened with them.

Eddie came back.

"Sir, we have something. We contacted Santa Cruz Trading. There is no Mr Tomoda. Apparently the owner is a Mr Naoyuki Sato. And yes, we have verification he left on a flight for Cebu in the Philippines the evening of the bombing. His phone was used and very near the bombing site. We are trying to locate him, not having much luck. There is no record of him after arriving in Cebu. Perhaps we should ask the Americans? They have very good contacts there."

"Yes, go ahead. Get Philip Barnes in here. We will need his help."

"Yes, Sir."

So now we had a tie-in. Tetsu Sato, Naoyuki Sato and Daisuke Tsuruyama"

"Eddie, I'll go to interview the Tsuruyamas now."

"Yes, Sir."

Waiting in the interview room were the Tsuruyamas. Ichiru was looking very angry. Hiroshi was looking at his cell-phone. Johnny Graham was stunned. Hiroshi was the spitting image of his grandfather. He stopped and looked again. Yes, it was incredible. They say characteristics skip generations but this was uncanny.

"Good morning, gentlemen. Sorry for the delay. We have been very busy following leads."

Ichiru Tsuruyama frowned and glared. "What is wrong with you Hong Kong police? Our Restaurant was bombed and you keep us in suspense. This is an outrage."

So much for the quiet and gentle post-war Japanese, Johnny Graham thought. "Well, Mr Tsuruyama Senior. I find that comment a bit offensive. Particularly since your family has lived here for so long under our care. I hasten to note that you do have a record with our police force for several rather big fights."

"Those were nothing. I never did anything. I was arrested and accused without reason. Now my restaurant is damaged. What is this about?"

"Mr Tsuruyama, we're following every lead. Do you have any problems or enemies which might lead to this action?"

"Nothing."

"Any gambling debts?"

"None. I spend a lot of time in China. We have never had any problems. Why is my restaurant still closed? I need to get in."

"We will check your restaurant later today," Johnny Graham replied, turning to the other man. "Mr Tsuruyama Junior. Do you have any enemies or problems or suspect anyone who might be involved in this bombing?"

"None that I know of." He spoke with a snarl, and a look of superiority. Johnny Graham had green eyes and they resented the question.

"Mr Tsuruyama Junior, you arrived in Hong Kong just a few years ago. Where were you raised?"

"I was raised in Japan, of course, in Hiroshima, which was the former home of my grandfather."

"You were raised by your mother?"

"Yes."

"Where did you study?"

"I studied at Tokyo University."

"I note an address in Kure on your Hong Kong Residence application."

"Yes, we also have a house in Kure. It was the home of my grandfather's father."

"Your grandfather is Daisuke Tsuruyama, correct?"

"Yes."

"What was his business?"

"He operated a trading company – Mount Niitaka Trading."

"I have information he was in Hong Kong during the war. Is that true?"

Ichiru Tsuruyama, the father, answered, "Yes. He was here in Hong Kong during the war."

"What was his post?"

"He was in the Japanese Navy. You know we conquered Hong Kong and most of China don't you?"

"Yes. I do. My grandfather was your guest in Stanley Internment Camp. So of course I know. So do all the Hong Kong Chinese and all the Mainland Chinese, which is why we find the idea of you insulting our Chinese police officers so outrageous."

"What does my father have to do with this?"

"I'm not sure. We are checking all leads. Does the name, Tetsu Sato mean anything to you?"

"No, I have never heard that name."

"Does the name Naoyuki Sato ring a bell?"

"No, I have never heard of them."

"Mr Tsuruyama Junior, have you ever heard of them?"

"No."

"Now, since you're from Kure and Hiroshima, why is the Restaurant named 'Matsushima Bay'?"

"Not really sure. Maybe my father knows."

Mr Tsuruyama Senior was getting really mad.

"It is just a name. We have tried for many years to provide good Japanese food there. Why is the name important?

"Just checking, Mr Tsuruyama. We need to check everything."

"Well, check then!"

"We will. Mr Tsuruyama, tell me about your travel to China. I see you make many trips there, to Dalian and Fujian and Beijing."

"I have business there. Is that wrong?"

"No. What kind of business?"

"We are always looking at factories and are trying to do investment. Nothing uncommon. I want to get into my restaurant as soon as possible. We have many valuables there. I must check on them."

"OK, Sir, we will let you back in as soon as we can. Thanks for your time. I'll be doing a final check of the restaurant today. We will need your finger-prints. Please go with Probationary Inspector Lo. He's waiting outside. We will inform you when you can re-enter the restaurant. I hope soon. Thanks for your cooperation."

They left with eyes glaring and almost bumped into Eddie when he came in to escort them for finger prints. The Tsuruyamas were bad news. Poor Hong Kong. What was going on?

He saw Mr Tanaka waiting outside. He called him in.

"Hello, Mr Tanaka."

"What do you have, Inspector? The Tsuruyamas were very upset at your delayed interview."

"Upset? Why, we're just doing our job. They seem to have problems."

"Well, I hope you're making progress?"

"Yes, we are. I'll need all the information you have on a Japanese national who is a possible suspect in this case."

Tanaka almost jumped. "A Japanese? How is that possible?"

"Well, I'm not sure. But I'll need the information quickly. Here is the information we have on the person, a Mr Naoyuki

Sato. He's from Sendai in Japan. Please try to investigate this. I'm trying to keep this out of the newspapers. I hope you understand. We expect your full cooperation."

"Yes, I'm shocked. Right away! When will you unseal the restaurant? The Tsuruyamas are very concerned about their property there."

"I'm sure they are. We have more inspections to do. Soon I hope."

"OK, I'll get on this right away." He departed in a shocked state, walking so fast, he was almost running, and calling someone with an urgent voice in Japanese as he was doing it.

When he got back to the operations centre, Philip Barnes, the American, was there.

"You sent for me, Johnny?"

"Well yes, Philip. There may be some tie-in to the Philippines."

"Yes, really?"

"Yes, we have a potential suspect who left that night for Cebu. Here's the information. Please see if you can get anything. We have no location after he left the airport.

"OK. I'm on it. But I'll need more cooperation with you for this."

"I know, Philip. I know."

"OK, be back soonest."

"Thanks, Philip."

The Chief Inspector came in. "Graham, what is this with the Japanese?"

He showed Chief Wong the evidence so far, and filled him in on the background. The Chief just sat there listening with a frown on his face.

"Well, this is a bit sensitive you know, especially the World War II tie-in. Very sensitive to all of us. We really do not like to drag up the past any more. We have many, many wonderful Japanese guests here every day.

"Yes, Chief, I know. But that's the evidence. Just letting you know."

"Yes, thank you. Keep me informed."

So that was it. Sensitive. Yesterday it was "Get this done now!" Today it was "Sensitive". What a mess! What was the deal with this Naoyuki guy? And the Tsuruyamas were bad news.

Johnny Graham decided to call Major Wu.

"Major Wu, meet me at the Discovery Bay Ferry Pier later today. I need to talk to you.

"Sure, I'll be there."

"Great! 3pm. We can walk and talk. Thanks."

"Good. Thanks."

He left and Eddie came back in.

"Eddie, did we get any prints on the postcards?"

"Yes, quite a few. All the same. Sir, I think this guy wants us to catch him."

"Yes, Eddie, really quite strange, all of it. It's giving me a headache, just thinking about it all."

"Very strange, I agree. You know, I had relatives killed by the Japanese in the war. This is a very strange case. I wish this was a case like the acid attack. We never caught the criminal, but we also never had to bring all this old stuff back. I don't like it at all.

"I'm not feeling too good about it either."

"Anyway, keep up the good fight. If this is where we must go, it is where we must go."

"Yes, Sir. The car is here. Where are you going?"

"Just out for a while, I'll be back later. I need to check on something. I'll call when it's time for the restaurant inspection. Also, see if the prints on the postcards are anywhere in the restaurant! Also, one of the reports indicated a big safe in the Tsuruyamas' office. Is that correct?"

"Yes, Sir. I saw the pictures. It is a very big safe. Both Tanaka and Mr Tsuruyama, the father, were asking about it and the damage to the restaurant, since you haven't let them in. Your car is here. When you will be back?"

"Soon, and thanks."

The car? Yes, where was he going? That was always the best question. Where was this going? He noticed the new day was grey but in the harbour he could see shafts of lights coming down from the sky. He put his sunglasses on, just to be inconspicuous. Johnny Graham couldn't think very well and almost tripped getting out of the car. Maybe it wasn't a good idea to bring the Chinese in on this. But Hong Kong was now China and there was no escaping it. Major Wu was waiting for him, also wearing sunglasses.

"Well, Major Wu. Sunglasses on a cold day! I guess in Sichuan you don't get to wear them often because of the mist."

"Yes, you're right, Inspector. In Chengdu, we're not used to seeing the sun. Very true. How do you know?"

"I'm just a simple student and I love the *Tale of Three Countries*. It has a lot of Chengdu in there."

"Yes? Really. It's a great book."

"Yes, one of Chairman Mao's favorites. You remember Chairman Mao don't you?"

"Yes, I have heard of him."

Major Wu was laughing. "You're a very strange policeman."

"Not that strange. I find it very strange that we have not met so far."

"But we have. I really like your new Toyota car. The license plate is HKXXXX, is it not?"

Now Johnny was laughing. "Well, Major Wu. Sorry, that's not my car. I borrowed it from a girl-friend last month. You guys need to work harder."

"OK, we will." Major Wu looked disappointed.

"Don't be sad, Major Wu. I even confuse myself. It's hard to follow someone who doesn't even know where he's going himself. I couldn't even follow this myself. And I have to give you credit about the case. You're very smart.

"Let's take the ferry! Not good, just standing here."

They boarded a cross-harbour ferry. He looked out at the grey green water of the harbour.

"Look, Major Wu, I don't like the Tsuruyamas. There's something very bad about them. I think you should check up on them.

"OK, I can look at that."

"Also, there's a big safe in the Restaurant. I think your people might want to check it. Both the Tsuruyamas were very concerned about it. I can arrange for your guys to get in tonight at about 12 midnight. How does that sound?"

"I'm very surprised at the offer. How can we get in?"

"I'll wait for you at the Cheung Kee noodle shop and give you the key to the back door. But your guys need to be good and quick. I'll need the key back. No prints."

"Yes, they will be efficient," Major Wu replied.

"After you check the place out, let me know. Please consider this my service to you."

"We will. Thanks a lot. We didn't expect such kindness."

"This is just part of my patriotic duty. Let's just keep it to ourselves. There is just something wrong with those guys."

"Thanks very much. We appreciate it."

"I appreciate the information about the battleship," Johnny reciprocated the thanks. "By the way, have you ever heard of Mount Niitaka? That was the name of the Tsuruyamas' Trading Company?"

"Yes, what bastards! Mount Niitaka is the Japanese name for Mount Yushan in Taiwan. During the Japanese Occupation it was the highest point in the Japanese Empire, even taller than Mount Fuji. In fact, when they launched the war against the British, Dutch and Americans, the Japanese used the signal, 'Climb Mount Niitaka'. These guys are incredible. Here in Hong Kong. Niitaka? As if we could ever forget. For you the war was five years. For us it started in 1895 when they took Taiwan and moved into Korea and Northern China. This was a generational conflict. We can never forget. I'm very angry at these two."

The Major was flushed with anger.

"OK, Major. I'll see you later. Please do a good job and cover your tracks. Nothing stolen or messed up, please!"

"You have my word and I truly thank you. It seems we never get help from anyone. You're the first foreigner to be so supportive."

"You forget, Major. We were allies in the war and you forget, I love China."

"Thanks again. See you tonight." Major Wu gave him a strange look and a smile and then was off into the city.

Johnny Graham was happy that he had helped. He didn't know what these guys were up to, maybe nothing. But China deserved some help with this. They had bent over backward about Taiwan which was very close to Japan. When the Chinese had taken over Hong Kong, there was a flock of boo birds shouting that this was the end. And yet, somehow, things were still functioning. They had gone out of their way to be professional and non-intrusive. This was amazing to Johnny. And yes, they were really nice guys sometimes. Most importantly, they now owed him, like he owed Big Rabbit and the blasted American. But the Americans wouldn't figure anything out. So they couldn't expect anything from him later, either. What a lovely game to be playing. Thank you, Mr Sato.

Matsushima Bay, the Restaurant

He went back to the Restaurant. It was his first trip back to the crime scene. The road was now open but the pavement was closed off. He was let in by a police constable.

The restaurant was not unusual. It was a nondescript typical Japanese restaurant. Some wooden tables, sake on the counter, and Japanese pictures. The only notable feature was the painting of a big mountain on the main wall. Of course, he already knew it was not Mount Fuji; but Mount Niitaka.

He went into the main office, which was quite large when considering the size of the restaurant. A chalkboard listed what appeared to be sailing-schedules of vessels in and out of China. And yes, the Tsuruyamas were really incredible. There was a picture of the "Matsushima City" – the battleship and another picture of an older man in naval uniform. It didn't look like Daisuke. It must have been the great-grandfather. These guys were a piece of work. Really, it was fine to have this kind of stuff in Japan, but here in Hong Kong? He guessed they must have felt pretty secure to be so blatant. There was a very big safe on the right side of the room.

"Sir?"

"Yes, Eddie."

"We have a match on the fingerprints on the main window. It looks like Sato has been here."

"Are there prints anywhere else?"

"No, just on the window, inside and outside."

"OK, log it down."

He sat down at the desk in the office and went through the files. Still more boat schedules, a couple of books in Japanese and three bottles of sake. He was not sure what was pertinent to the case any more. He was confused and all he wanted to do was go home and watch some commercials.

"Eddie, close the street tonight from midnight. I'll prepare another final inspection then. Tomorrow you can unseal the restaurant.

"Yes, Sir."

When he got back to the office, he found Tanaka waiting in the hallway.

"Mr Graham, I just came back to tell you that we're working on this for you. Still nothing. The first information is that Mr Sato is a very successful businessman. We have no evidence of any wrong-doing in the past. We are very sorry about this."

"Yes, I know you are. I'm keeping this out of the papers for now for you. Apparently we do have Mr Sato's prints at the crime scene. We need your help in finding him. He took a plane to the Philippines.

"We're going to mount a search at his flat in a little while. Hopefully something will turn up. Apparently he's a bit of a loner, and is almost never in the office. He's known as a contributor to politicians. Apparently he's very rich. Other than that we don't have much to give you."

"I'll report back soon. We appreciate your calm and quiet attitude about this."

"Well, I'm trying to work with you, Mr Tanaka. I know these things can be sensitive."

"Thank you, thank you so much."

Mr Tanaka left, this time running and talking on his cell-phone. So much for Buddhism and Shinto. This was panic. Poor guy. It was turning out to be a bad day for the Japanese team this year.

"Eddie, I need to go. It's that time."

"Yes, I know, Sir."

He thought Eddie was looking at his scar.

Disorientation: The Science of Life and Mr Sato

It was time to check out. He could never finish anything. Even though the case was reaching its zenith, it was time for him to check out. Everyone has their excuses, for every fault, and every mistake. Johnny Graham had his.

His excuse began during a bad typhoon in 1996. He had chosen the wrong time to get drunk and take his family out in the car and lose his temper. He was yelling at his wife and banging the steering wheel when he failed to see the brake lights on the car in front of him. The result was a massive car accident. His wife and three-year-old daughter were dead and he was left with a big scar on his face.

Scars are funny things. There are outer scars and inner scars. We all have some. Outer scars are different. People will do anything not to look at our outer scars. They purposely avert their eyes, and do anything not to mention them. We are repulsed by outer ugliness and will strive to avoid the sight of it. Johnny Graham always considered his outer scar a blessing. Because people were trying so hard to avoid looking at his outer scar they would be less likely to see his inner scar.

After the accident, Johnny had been in a near coma for about two weeks. He didn't even remember his wife and his daughter for another ten days. When it hit him, the grief and the loss was incredible. He could not deal with it. He could not believe, nor forgive what he had done.

He then tried to kill himself. Of course, this didn't work.

Johnny Graham had suffered what we call a mental breakdown or mental collapse. He spent all of 1997, the Year of the Ox, in treatment, and using a wide range of anti-depressant drugs. It was a lost year, one he could not even remember.

Chief Inspector Wong had been kind and let him off the drunk-driving charge. They thought he had suffered enough.

Graham was clear however. He could never suffer enough for his stupidity. He could live a hundred lives and never obscure the stupidity of his grave mistake. No matter what drugs he took, or what the counselors told him; he knew he was condemned to suffer and grieve and never erase this terrible mistake.

He knew he had to figure something out. But it was impossible to find his way through the mist. He struggled and struggled. Day after day. How could he go on in this life? How could one live after destroying his own family? He thought of suicide again.

One day during a trip to China, on a cold misty winter day in Chengdu on Renmin Nan Lu, he finally figured it out. He was walking and looked intently at the blue cloth shoes of an old man. He could see the shoes and the grey sidewalk. He then looked to his left and saw an old man sitting next to a garbage cart. He was getting ready to read a green-covered book and putting on his glasses. It was suddenly so clear.

It was his science of life.

The key concept was disorientation. Johnny Graham finally understood that we're always in and out of disorientation, and refocusing.

Every time we enter a new room we must refocus to the new location.

Every time we hear a sound we must refocus to hear it.

Every time we see someone on the street we must refocus.

When we talk to someone we must focus on what they say and then prepare a response.

Every time we walk we must refocus on the sidewalk.

When we cross the street, we must look to left and right.

When we wake up from sleep, we refocus on our room and place and leave our sleep.

We do these minor movements every minute.

We look up and look down. We stop and start again.

We stand up and sit down.

We look at the rear view and side mirror when driving.

We are always in one place or another, or in another state of mind. We are constantly changing direction and focus. We are constantly in a state of disorientation moving from one thing to another. Looking here and then thinking that, moving our hands and legs, listening to this and that. It never ends.

The only way to avoid some of this is to be deaf, dumb, blind or mute. Or stay in one room and never go out and never eat and never talk to someone or never watch TV. Or to be dead.

It was all so simple. If there are 1,440 minutes in a day and night and 86,400 seconds, then how much time do we spend in this state of disorientation and refocusing? Is it half the time or the majority of the time? How much time do we really concentrate on anything? We are happy one minute and then our mood changes again. We never rest. Our mind is always moving and seeing something new.

It was clear. He knew it all then. It was clear, he could never grieve constantly. Disorientation would never stop. He knew he had to give the memory of his wife and daughter some time every day. He knew he had to grieve every day. But it could never be all the time.

As long as he dedicated some time every day, he could go on. That is what they would have wanted. If the accident had never happened they would have loved him as much and forgiven him for anger on the rainy night. They were gone, but they would live in him at least some of the time, interspersed between the disorientation of every day. The seconds lost all the time as we look, listen and move, would protect his daily life and he would give them the time they deserved until his life itself had ended.

After that day in Chengdu, he was fine. Chief Inspector Wong let him back on the force and he began again his life as a policeman.

He took his several minutes. He cried. He saw his loving wife and precious child. He remembered their smiles and love, the softness of their embrace and felt their breath on his cheek and could hear their hearts beating near to him. His wife was smiling like she would when he did something stupidly funny and his daughter was holding his hand once again. They were alive for just that minute, so alive. His mistake could be rectified for one minute. One minute of feeling was worth weeks of life. One second of purity and concentration meant more than a life-time of disorientation.

Amazingly enough after all that time lost and terrible suffering and confusion, Johnny Graham and his science of life led a renewed life. Because he understood disorientation, he became a much better policeman. Criminals were just people living deeply in disorientation. They were like ghosts trapped at one end of a bridge. They were confused and unable to cross the line. They lashed out by robbing, or fighting or killing. They were so deeply disorientated they could never find their way.

Since Johnny Graham had been to hell and back, he was that much better at understanding them and penetrating their inner scar. Since he was scarred for life, he did much better at understanding them because they were scarred too.

Yes, the outer scar was a blessing, but the inner scar was his salvation and his coat of armour.

He sat down in a coffee-shop for a rest.

What he could never figure out was the randomness of life itself. Why that night and that moment to slam the steering wheel? Why such a mistake? Why this pattern of life?

He looked out on the ships in the harbour and tried somehow to discern a pattern in the moving vessels. What was the rate of movement of each boat, and force of the water? Why did this boat go there and another boat there? How did they avoid hitting each other? It looked so random and yet worked so well as if unseen hands with spread fingers were pushing each one in the correct course which would prevent mishap. It was a miracle that was unseen and not understood. It was randomness. He still had not figured it out. He would continue to search for an answer to that one.

On to Mr Sato.

Well what were you doing, Mr Sato?

It was an obvious case of disorientation in a severe way. Or maybe he was just graduating from his affliction. He had worked so hard to give them the clues. He really had it in for the Tsuruyamas.

Johnny Graham was sure that he would soon find out. The case was being solved not by him, but by Sato himself. He was sure that Sato would leave somehow and somewhere the final clue for all of them. He felt it was coming soon.

The "Kumano": Final Days

The "Kumano" Chronology Continued

8 July 1944:
CruDiv 7's "KUMANO", SUZUYA, TONE and CHIKUMA are loaded with troops and supplies. They depart Kure with Group "A": BatDiv 1's YAMATO and MUSASHI, CruDiv 4's ATAGO, TAKAO, MAYA and CHOKAI and Des Ron 2's light cruiser NOSHIRO and her destroyers. Group A is accompanied by Group "B": Bat Div 1's NAGATO, Bat Div 3's KONGO, Cru Div 7's MOGAMI and DesRon 10's light cruiser YAHAGI and her destroyers.

10 July 1944:
Arrives at Okinawa. Group A detaches from Group B and departs Okinawa.

16 July 1944:
Arrives at Singapore, offloads troops and supplies.

17 July 1944:
Proceeds to Lingga (S. of Singapore) to join the Mobile Fleet.

18 October 1944:
Vice Admiral Shirashi's CruDiv 7 departs Lingga in Vice Admiral Kurita's First Raiding Force with Vice Admiral Susuki Yoshio's Force "B" (Northern Force): BatDiv 3's KONGO and HARUNA and DesRon 10's YAHAGI and destroyers NOWAKI, KIYOSHIMA, URAKAZE, YUKIFAZE, HAMAKAZE, and ISOKAZE.

20 October 1944:
Arrives at Brunei Bay, Borneo.

22-26 October 1944 Operation "SHO-I-GO"
(Victory) - The Battle of Leyte Gulf.
Departs Brunei for Leyte Gulf via the San
Bernardino Strait.

25 October 1944: The Battle off Samar
While attacking Task Force 77. 4.3's "Jeep"
Carriers, "KUMANO" is hit by a torpedo from
destroyer USS JOHNSTON (DD-557). The Mark 15
tears a section of "KUMANO"'s bow off. She
retires toward the San Bernardino Strait at 15
knots, but is attacked by Task Force 38
torpedo and dive-bombers and damaged by a near
miss.

26 October 1944:
Sibuyan Sea. "KUMANO" is attacked by aircraft
from the USS HANCOCK (CV-19) and hit by three
500-lb bombs. She is ordered to proceed to
Coron Bay and is joined by ASHIGARA and
destroyer USHIO. Refuels from oiler NICHEI
MARU.

27-28 October 1944:
Departs Coron for Manila with OKINAMI.

28 October-3 November 1944:
Manila. Emergency repairs are performed on her
bow and four boilers.

29 October 1944:
Manila. "KUMANO" and NACHI are attacked by
Task Force 38's Carrier Planes.

4 November 1944:
At 0100, departs Manila for TAKAO, Formosa
with AOBA in convoy MATA-31 with six
freighters, two kaibokan coast defence
frigates and five sub-chasers. After they

depart Manila, is raided by Task Force 58 and many ships are sunk or damaged.

5 November 1944:
At 10,000 yards, convoy MATA-31 (15 ships with air cover) is spotted by lookouts aboard Cdr (later Rear Admiral) John K. Fyfes' USS BATFISH (SS-310). Fyfe makes a submerged approach on AOBA under the escorts, but when he comes to periscope depth, BATFISH is almost rammed by a destroyer. Fyfe aborts his approach and crash-dives. Later, he fires six torpedoes at a large cargo ship, but they all miss.

6 November 1944:
Cape Bolinao, Luzon. The convoy is attacked by a wolf-pack composed of Lt Cdr (later Captain) Enrique D. Haskins' USS GUITARRO (SS-363), LtCdr W. G. Chapple's BREAM (SS-243), LtCdr Maurice W. Shea's RATON (SS-270) and LtCdr William T. Kinsella's RAY (SS-271). GUITARRO, BREAM and RAY share credit for sinking the 6,800-ton transport KAGA MARU.

The four submarines fire 23 torpedoes at "KUMANO". At 1052, she is hit by two torpedoes. One blows off her repaired bow section. The second hits near her starboard engine-room. All four engine-rooms flood. She takes on an 11 degree list to starboard and becomes unnavigable. At 1930, "KUMANO" is taken under tow by DORYO MARU to Dasol Bay.

7 November 1944:
At 1500, arrives in Santa Cruz, Luzon.

7-20 November 1944:
Santa Cruz harbour. Undergoes emergency repairs by personnel brought up from the Manila Repair Facility.

25 November 1944:
"KUMANO" is attacked by aircraft from Task Force 38's USS TICONDEROGA (CV-14). She is hit by five torpedoes and four 500-lb bombs. At 1515, "KUMANO" capsizes and sinks in 108 feet of water in Santa Cruz harbour at 15-45N, 119-48E. Five hundred and ninety-five survivors are rescued, but Captain Hitomi is killed. He is promoted to Rear-Admiral, posthumously.

Let There Be Light

Johnny Graham went back to the office. That time was over. Back to work. When at work only be at work.

He took more time to study the cruiser, "Kumano". The cruiser had been in most of the war, serving in numerous battles. He checked the date; 7 July 1944. He found nothing for that date. Apparently it had been in dry dock for a couple of weeks. On the 8th of July it had left Kure and moved back to action. It had sailed in a Battle Group to Singapore to unload troops on the 16th of July. Then it had departed for Brunei, which was the last major oil source for the Japanese Empire. On the 22nd of October 1944 it had joined with the First Raiding Force under Admiral Kurita to launch an attack against the American Navy massing for the invasion of the Philippines off Leyte.

The First Raiding Force had gone through the San Bernardino Strait and hooked south off the Island of Samar to do battle with American Forces. On the 25th of October, just as the Battle off Samar was beginning, the "Kumano" had been hit by a torpedo fired from a submarine. Her front bow was almost blown off and she left the battle heading back to Manila. On the 26th of October, in the Sibuyan Sea she was hit again, this time by bombs dropped from planes from an American air-craft carrier. She was heavily damaged and was towed by a freighter to Manila. From the 28th of October to the 4th of November, the "Kumano" was in Manila harbour undergoing rushed emergency repairs. On the 4th of November, she departed Manila, with the destination Takeo port in Taiwan. On the 6th of November, while cruising the coast off Luzon, she was attacked again by an American submarine wolf-pack. Two torpedoes hit and did extensive damage, re-destroying her damaged bow area, and flooding all the engine-rooms. She was towed again to Santa Cruz harbour in Zambales province, where she underwent more repairs from the 7th to the 20th of November, during which time she was ripped from her moorings by a typhoon. An further rushed repair was completed and on the 25th of November the "Kumano" headed out to sea again.

Her luck ran out on this date. She was hit by five 500-pound bombs and four or five more torpedoes from an American Air Attack Squadron. She sank in Dasol Bay off Santa Cruz Harbour in the afternoon of November 25th 1944. Half the remaining crew died in the blasts or were strafed in the water by American planes.

He quickly checked Sato's date of birth. He was born in April 1945. If Testsu Sato had died on the "Kumano", Naoyuki Sato had never known his father, a clear indication of severe and complete disorientation in life. Johnny Graham should know. He was the expert on being out of place and lost. Too bad he never knew Naoyuki before. He might have been able to help him before he made his big mistake. This is what bothered him. Randomness. Naoyuki and randomness, Johnny Graham and randomness. The world in its perfect randomness.

He checked the map of the Philippines. Both Leyte and the Sibuyan Sea were near Cebu. Maybe Sato was there off Samar, or . . .? − Santa Cruz Zambales was about four hours from Manila.

"Eddie, did that American come back?"

"No, Sir."

"Did Tanaka come back?"

"No, Sir."

"Please call them…. We're still waiting for any information on Sato. This is urgent."

"Yes, Sir."

"OK. Thanks Eddie, I'll be out again now. Back about 1am."

"Yes, Sir."

Johnny Graham checked his watch. It was 11.30pm. He had to hurry to meet up with Major Wu.

As planned, Major Wu was waiting for him in the Cheung Kee noodle shop. He looked anxious and excited. He looked too much the part, with a black leather jacket and black shoes and slacks. He was too excited, like a teenager before his first kiss. This was a special night for Major Wu.

"We are ready; please give us the keys," Major Wu said.

"Sure, here they are. Make sure you leave no prints and that nothing is moved. The safe is in the office. I've never seen such a large safe in a restaurant. Be back in an hour. The street will be reopened soon. I have to give the restaurant back to the Tsuruyamas tomorrow. So this is your last easy chance."

"I hope we can trust you, Inspector Graham."

"You had better trust me. You know the English saying: 'Never look a gift horse in the mouth.'"

"Yes, I do. Yes, you are our gift horse. Thank you."

With that, he rushed off into the night. From the noodle shop window he could see Major Wu and three black-clad men rush into the alley behind the restaurant. Graham calmly ordered his favourite won-ton noodles and a plate of vegetables. He looked down at a white formica table and saw the steam rising from his bowl of noodles. The long vegetable spinach was a brilliant electric green colour, and the soup itself was a golden tan.

While he was eating, all he could think of was the letters "HTK". What had Sato meant by these letters? "HTK"? Was it important to the case or not? "HTK...HTK...HTK...."

He decided just to enjoy his noodles. The mysterious "HTK" could wait.

Immaculate Heart

At that same time in Sendai Japan, Chiasa Honda could not sleep. She had just vomited and her period was late. She was trying to calculate the last time she had been with Naoyuki.

Calculating the days of a woman's menstrual cycle when the period is late is one of the hardest things to do in life, for some reason. Suddenly dates are impossible to remember. She could not remember when her last period had ended nor when she had been with him last time. Was it two weeks ago or three weeks ago or was it twelve days ago? This event and its time in relation to her last period were jumbled endlessly in her mind.

There is always that, "Oh, no! Is this possible?" mixed with a "What will our child be like?" mixed with a, "Should I have it?" and a "Can I handle a baby?" Then there is always the "How should I tell him?" and "How will he react?"

There are over four billion of us on this planet. And there have been over four billion of these moments, the quiet almost frightened thoughts of our mothers when they first knew that they were pregnant. Somewhere in every city and town and valley in the world a woman is thinking these things every day of every year.

The first thoughts of a newly pregnant woman are one of the most delicate moments of life itself. This is where our relationship with our mothers begins. Our relationship with our fathers begins when our mother tells them. Our mother is the first to feel our existence and the first to recognize the future.

Sometimes these first thoughts are happy, sometimes they are sad and worried, but these thoughts are the beginning of our relationship with our mothers and our relationship with the world itself, for it is through our mother that we gain access to all.

Each case, life and relationship, are of course different to some extent. In her case Chiasa was not sure what Naoyuki would say. After all, he was married, and often away. He was not young any more and had children from his other wife.

He never spoke of this other family. It was strange, almost as if they didn't exist. Or maybe he was just being polite so as not to hurt her feelings. No woman wants to hear about another woman being with her man. But hardly a word did he say in all these years. She didn't even know how many children he had or where he lived. One time he had said he lived in Tokyo, then another time he said that he had lived in the "Kumano", near Hiroshima. Once he had said he wanted to live in the Philippines, that he had some relatives there. She didn't think much about all this. It was just not pertinent to their love. She never pressured him and he never asked for their love to be anything more than what it was. They just lived. When they were together there was something there, a feeling. Maybe a child would be alright with him?

Two people are always two people. But two people can be tied together. She felt this with Naoyuki and her child. They were tied together forever. They were tied like clouds are tied to the sea and pass over the earth pushed by the wind. They were tied like the leaves in autumn that float down from the tree as the first bite of winter brings them to the ground. They were tied like shadows are tied to the light that creates them. There was just something there as there had always been for lovers since the dawn of man. They were tied by the feelings of ten years and the knowledge that ten years is the same as a hundred or a thousand years. There was no break between them even if he was somewhere else and she was here alone in the night thinking about him and hoping he was well wherever he might be.

Unlike her last pregnancy, and the tragic loss of her child, and cruelty of her tough previous boyfriend, she was sure that this baby would live. She would guard this child even with her life. Loss would be turned to life. The Protector Jizo would be there for her this time. Only the Jizo knew what she had suffered before. At that time she had no-one else to turn to.

In the dark of the night, she felt that whisper of love, like the sound of a soft summer rain, or the sound of wind through the pines of Matsushima. This was the call of life and she would follow that sound, whatever might come. This is what she promised herself.

She would always feel like this, tonight especially and forever. She was suddenly happy as if knowing that forever was now, and their child was a step in the direction of forever. She could believe in this, and now she could rest despite the soft pain in her womb and an upset stomach. It was from this sweet pain that her child would come.

Alone with these thoughts and the child in her womb, Chiasa finally fell asleep in the warmth of her bed.

Noodles and Gunboats on the Yangtse River

The hour given to Major Wu was to be only forty minutes. He came back to the noodle shop and greeted Graham and sat down while handing him the keys.

"Why don't you have some noodles, Major Wu?"

"Sure, and I thank you."

"No need, I don't want to know anything. This never happened."

"Sure, I understand. Why did you help us?"

"Well it is a long story and it is our mutual story. I have lived here in Hong Kong all my life. And all my life has been under the shadow of China. I'm a child of our past relationship with China and have thought a lot about this. The war with Japan started for us in 1941, but for you it started in 1895, as Japan slowly started carving their own empire out of China and Korea. You saw the picture of the battleship in the Tsuruyamas' office, I assume."

Major Wu grimaced. "Yes. I could not believe it."

"Yes, that's my point. We in the West allowed the Japanese to attack China and never said a word. We were doing the same thing, carving China up into spheres of influence. Then we were so surprised and outraged when the Japanese attacked us. It was hypocrisy. We treated you poorly in your worst moment. I'm truly sorry and hope this little gesture will help you forgive our insensitive past. I cannot make the stupidity and double standards disappear, but I owe you all this much."

"Well, I appreciate the kindness now. We cannot change the past, but perhaps we can do better with our mutual futures. I thank you for understanding."

"Thank you also for every kindness and your understanding."

He was eating in that very Asian style, totally focused on his soup and yet somehow somewhere else in thought. They didn't say another word until Major Wu got up.

"Thanks for the soup and Japanese food today. We need to work on this unexpected gift."

"You're always welcome."

"Stay in touch."

"I will, Mr Wu."

Truth, Crimson Red and Cotton White

He knew now it was all a mistake. He had known before, of course.

Mistakes in life are like plagues. How they infect us we never know. A short moment of anger, an unkind comment, a flash of selfishness can bring an eternity of regret and hard feelings. Sometimes we don't even register our greatest mistakes for a very long time. But this was different.

Naoyuki Sato was beginning to die. The pills were beginning to take deadly effect on his body. It was getting cold, and there was no bright light to be seen. It was just cold. It was colder than he had ever felt in his life. Death is nothing more than that. Your body temperature drops along with the end of your beating heart. He was here in a very warm place, freezing. It was the end.

He had known it was a big mistake when he planted the bomb. IIc had known it was a big mistake when he had held Chiasa in their final embrace. – The last time they could ever be together. – It had felt so special. He didn't know why. He had known it was a mistake as he left her apartment, without saying goodbye to the love of his life, sleeping quietly on the bed under the blanket decorated with small brown, cute and smiling bear cubs. He had known it was a mistake when he took the plane to Hong Kong to commit his final act.

When we make mistakes we often just excuse them to ourselves. "I had no choice. I did this because of this. I really had to. My cruel words were just a reflex. You would not feel so bad if only you understood why I did this to you." This is how we excuse our crimes. We each have one thousand mistakes to atone for, and each one has its own excuse.

Naoyuki could do this too. And yes even his excuse had some line of reason.

It was April 20th 1964, at 6.30pm, three weeks after his birthday.

He had just received his college entrance exam results and told his mother that he wanted to join the Japanese Self Defence Force, to keep up the military tradition in his family and honour his father, who had died in November 1944 aboard the Japanese cruiser, the "Kumano".

Her reaction was the biggest shock of his entire life. She had turned from the quiet silent caring mother he knew into a monster. For the first time she had screamed.

"No! Never! I forbid you!"

She had screamed. She had thrown the plates off the dinner table. She had threatened to beat him. Her eyes were wild and violent.

"I will never allow you to ruin your life with those that killed your father."

She screamed every bad word in the Japanese language. She became a demon.

"Never, Naoyuki! Never will I allow it."

She broke every bowl in the house.

Naoyuki didn't know what had hit him

"Why, Mother? What have I done?"

"Can't you see anything? We have lived in hell because of them. I lost everything. My life was destroyed when he died. He was everything to me. Because of them your father lies in his watery grave, alone without us. Those animals did this. There was no honour in the end. We were defeated and yet they sent more and more to die. Your father was a god living within the confines of hell, surrounded by beasts like Tsuruyama."

"Tsuruyama? Who is that?"

"Tsuruyama." He had never even heard that name before. His mother began to cry. And not just cry. The torrents of tears embraced the whole apartment. She cried like an insane person. She cried uncontrollably, endlessly, for hours.

Sometimes she stopped briefly to break more plates, sometimes she collapsed and tore her hair.

Naoyuki never knew what hit him. He shook with each tear. His mouth was dry. His world was destroyed. His mother was suddenly so cruel to him. Where there had been love was only rage in its final form.

Then it ended.

"Naoyuki, I'll tell you more tomorrow. Please help me clean up."

With that, the storm had passed. He would never see her rage again. She would never raise her voice again in life. She returned to the stoic person he had always known. It was the first and last time she would be like this. The demon had entered her and left. She was back.

But the appearance of the demon did something to him. He knew she had passed her hate and anger to his soul in one astounding moment. His very death and existence for the next thirty years was determined on that night. She had changed him and his world. She had coloured his eyes with the grey of death and the black of hate in one moment.

Whether that was her one mistake or not, he would never know. But it had led to his own final mistakes, as surely as the moon will block the sun during an eclipse. But this eclipse never ended. The sight of his mother's collapse that night removed the sun from his world forever.

The next day, his world was turned over.

"Naoyuki, I really have never told you about this. I really never planned to tell you. Yesterday, the thought of you joining the Self Defence Forces brought back something I had buried deep in my soul, ever since the last time I saw your father alive.

With that she bowed before the picture of his father in a small shrine. Then she went to a box under her bed and took out a big photo album; one he had never seen before.

"It is time you know. I will tell you this story only once. Do not ask me about this again. We will never discuss this another time. But I must tell you now."

She reached into the photos and put one of his father in his hands.

"Your father, Tetsu Sato. Yes, you know who he is. You have been looking at his picture every day of your life at our small shrine near the kitchen. But you do not know who he was. It is my mistake that I have never told you. But I could not do so. Now I must so you can understand what happened here last night.

"Your father was a prince. He was my god. He was the greatest man a woman could ever know. He's gone now for almost twenty years but I never spent one minute without thinking about him. I promised I would love him forever and I have kept my word. I promised him that if he didn't return I would not show my grief and that I would raise you in peace and love. I did this until last night and now I must live with my failure to keep this promise.

"He was, as you know, a naval officer in the Japanese Imperial Fleet. He died as you know aboard the cruiser, "Kumano" in the late November of 1944, when the "Kumano" was sunk by the Americans. These things you know.

"What you do not know, Naoyuki, is that he was the Honour Graduate of the Class of 1935 at the Etajima Military Academy. You do not know that he was sent to England to study with the British Navy after graduation and that he could speak perfect English, as one day I hope you will do. This would honour him. You do not know that he was perfect and civilized. He was able and capable of meeting any challenge. He was kind and a devout Buddhist. He never said one unkind word and was gentle to each and all. I'm so sorry that you've never met anyone who knew him, because they would all say the same. I was more than lucky to have been his wife. How I was ever so blessed I will never know. But blessed I was. And you are blessed to be his son as I am blessed to be your mother. I see much of you in him. But our lives are never that of our parents and I have failings also, though I must admit I never saw one fault from your father. I am to blame for any faults you may have, he is not.

"Your father, had he lived, would never have reacted the way I did last night. He was proud to fight for Japan and the Emperor during the war. He was willing to die. He would not oppose you joining the Self Defence Forces. But I forbid it.

"This is my sin.

"Each story has a beginning and an end. As your mother I know when your life began.

"Your father and I were together for a short time from the 26th of June 1944 to the 7th of July 1944, when the 'Kumano' came back for repairs at the Kure Naval Base. We had our last time together then. It was the last moments of love in our lives together. You were born nine months after this short time. I had not seen him since October 1943, as he was away fighting for almost one year.

"This trip he was changed. He told me the war was lost. Of course we all knew it was bad. Every day there were funerals and crying. The Americans were coming closer. But we all told ourselves that perhaps this would change. One great victory was all it would take. Your father knew better, he had been in many battles by then. He had just been in a great battle and had seen what the Americans could do. Many of our ships and aircraft carriers were damaged and the American submarines were everywhere. Though the "Kumano" had not been seriously damaged, your father knew that it was just a matter of time. He was not going to avoid telling me the truth again, as he had done before. It was just a fact that he might not survive.

"It didn't dim our love at all. Nor did it dim the spirit of our country. We thought just maybe we could prevail. I told your father this, one night under a full moon. He smiled sadly. No, he told me, this was not going to end well. But he would do his best to survive and return to me. He knew already we were defeated and a new world was coming to Japan. He told me he accepted the new world and if he could return would humbly embrace our defeat as he had embraced our past victories. But, if he could never see the new world he would accept that also.

"By the last day, I thought I might be pregnant. I told him. He cried. We cried together. He asked me to promise him you would be brought up in peace and love. I promised him that we – you and I, Naoyuki – would be here waiting for him the next time he returned. It was both our happiest and saddest time together. How can you say a true good-bye when you know in your heart you will never see someone again? How can you say good-bye when it might not be the final good-bye? How can you ever really say good-bye? I'm sure we both were not sure, and at the same time we both knew.

"We say good-bye every day. We say good-bye to another day. We say good-bye to night when we wake. We say constant good-byes to those we have never known and those we pass on the street. What makes me most sad, Naoyuki, is knowing that I never had the chance to say good-bye to your father. For these past twenty years, when you see me leave at night to go to the ocean, I am saying good-bye. I will do this until I die, because I never got the chance to tell him when he was so close to me. This is the horror of my life and it started on that day.

"Naoyuki, that day was really very busy, there were many activities at the port and your father had to go later at night to board the "Kumano". There were many, many ships in the harbour, all with a feeling of action, as the Fleet prepared to leave. We stopped at a nearby restaurant to have a quiet meal together.

"This was our first mistake. All would have been so much better if we had not gone there. It was the Matsushima restaurant owned by a Naval Academy classmate of your father's. He liked the food, he said, though the food was not like our Sendai food. He thought it was funny, because the restaurant was really named after the battleship 'Matsushima

Bay' and not our dear Matsushima Bay near Sendai. I never thought much of it. In the far wall was a painting of Mount Niitaka, which was in Formosa now Taiwan. We sat down and ordered a simple meal.

"In a rear room, there was a loud drunken party going on. I realized then that we should leave. It was strange. I felt something bad was going to happen even then. But we had already ordered our food and it was too late to leave just then. Maybe I was anxious that our last night would be ruined. I was just suddenly very uncomfortable.

"After a few minutes, the drunken party was getting louder and louder. It was clear our quiet night was being ruined. But at that point I didn't know how ruined it would be. At a moment like that, with the world in turmoil, and death at the door-step of all of us, I just wanted to live in the last silence of that last meal with your father before our fleet left again toward an uncertain future. It was a natural desire of a pregnant woman and her love. I live in pain every day because of that night in the restaurant.

"Our food had not even arrived when out of the drunken room appeared a man with a long black leather coat. – I barely recognized him. But he recognized us. In the darkness of the hallway appeared Daisuke Tsuruyama. This was your father's friend from the Naval Academy. How they ever became friends, I never knew. He was everything your father was not. He was not polite or soft. He was rough and violent with bright eyes like a snake. He had not one soft bone in his body. Full of crude words and always looking for a fight.

"I had to tolerate him several times in the years with your father. I never knew what your father saw in him. I told him that Daisuke was a bad man, but your father said he had to maintain contacts from his Academy days.

"But sometimes you know when there is an enemy in the room. I knew Daisuke really hated your father despite the smiles and pats on the back. I was not sure what caused this hate because he was from a very successful naval family. Daisuke's father was one of the heads of the Kure Naval District and had served on the battleship "Matsushima Bay" in the war of 1895 against the Chinese and was considered a hero of the Battle of the Straits of Tsushima where we defeated the Russians in 1905. But the son is never the same as the father, as you are not the same as your father. He was bad. That is all I knew.

"Of course, that night he was drunk. He was not leaving with the fleet. Instead of fleet duty he had become part of the Japanese Naval Intelligence. He had served in Hong Kong and China, and had come back a very wealthy man. I asked your father about this sudden wealth in 1943 when we had seen Daisuke once. Your father looked at me in a puzzled way, like he had never considered it strange. He was like that, so unsuspecting of evil, so pure and on this night so mistaken."

Her hands were trembling, again. Like the night before.

"Daisuke then embraced your father and dragged us as his guests into the back room. I tried to dissuade him but he roughly grabbed us both in his big black hands and pushed us into the room. He was so drunk and violent I could smell the sickly odour of alcohol from the distance of the room.

"That room was hell itself. It was very large with about ten tough looking men and eight or so geishas all so very drunk. The men all looked like Daisuke, big, brawny and with leather jackets which were the favourite of the Kempetai, our special police. They looked like some sort of rough animals laughing and drinking.

"Daisuke seated us and began to brag about his exploits in China. Yes, we were winning the war there. The Chinese could never defeat us. He boasted that killing a Chinese meant nothing to them. The more they killed the better. He was a beast. The Geishas laughed and praised him as he threw money at them. One hundred million of us could defeat the world. He never asked your father how things were.

"Then he began to show us pictures, smuggled back from China and Hong Kong. They were disgusting. Pictures of death and murder. He bragged and bragged, while showing us pictures of beheaded Chinese, and British prisoners at the point of starvation. He said he loved the war, and could never get enough of it.

"The pictures were beyond imagination, and I felt sick. Naoyuki, these were the pictures I saw on your first days of life. I was repulsed beyond imagination. Maybe I was too emotional, but the sheer violence and bullying nature of this man and his friends made me ill. I began to cry, and your father tried to protect me from seeing the horror of these pictures.

"Daisuke would have none of it. He thrust more pictures right before my eyes as his monstrous friends laughed loudly and drunkenly. The monsters and the geishas were screaming at us to see the pictures. They were screaming 'Look, Look, Look!' There was no shame in the world that they would not condone. I had never seen such evil and not one day passes that I do not see them.

"You know I never say much. That night, they took my voice away. Better never to speak again than share a common language with such animals, better to be alone forever than share a world with such evil.

"Your father pushed him back. Daisuke swore at him and his friends pounced like wolves, beating your father and pushing me. Your father could do nothing, there was blood from his face and more blood streaked on his white naval uniform.

"Somehow this went on for a bit and then we were thrown on the street by the thugs and Daisuke Tsuruyama.

"Soon the Naval Police came and – with Daisuke shouting – they dragged your father off to the Fleet.

"I was stunned, beaten and crying as he was led away.

My last sight of him was the blood on the white of his uniform and blood on his pants. He could not look back to see me. The Naval police were forcing him away from me for this eternity, for this life of silence and pain. I never knew what we did to deserve such punishment in this life, or why the demon Daisuke Tsuruyama came into our path.

"That was our good-bye, Naoyuki. That was the end of my life. I walked the streets of Kure in pain that night and heard the horns of the Fleet as it departed. Only the moon was there to protect me and it was my moon of pain. As the Fleet left I died. But you were with me, for that I lived. You were part of him, Naoyuki. You were all I had left of my Tetsu. I had to live for him and for you.

"Of course, of course, the end was near. That night made it so obvious. The hell I had seen that night was the end of the war. I had seen both the good and the evil. The evil was so incredible. We had fallen so low, below the level of animals. The good was beaten and bloodied like your father. Red Blood on pure white cotton. What honour could have been his had been stolen by men like Daisuke Tsuruyama. I honestly believed that our Fleet was doomed by that one act of evil in that restaurant.

"Why we love such suffering I will never understand. But as the dawn came and the "Kumano" was out to sea, I knew life was over. And it was. Within two months your father was dead, though of course I did know it. The Americans moved with skill and soon the bombing of Japan began in earnest. It was the end. The end of your father was for me the end of Japan.

"We never knew exactly what happened to him and the "Kumano". We only found out much later that she was sunk in the Philippines. They announced the sinking in January 1945. But it was still so obvious.

"It was impossible to declare victory any more, while the Americans bombed us with fire from the sky. Our Japanese wooden houses could not withstand the fire. The Kamikaze fighters could never stem the tide. There was death and destruction everywhere. The World was turned to fire. And your eyes as an infant, Naoyuki, saw the fire. I could not bring you peace as I promised your father.

"It was our Armageddon, the end of the world. It was the world Daisuke Tsuruyama made for you, me and your father on that summer night. It was the world you were born into just before our final defeat. They took our purity, they took our love and left only the wet disgraced ashes of life itself.

"I'm so sorry, I'm so sorry that I had to tell you this today. I think you will understand now why I forbid you to join the Self Defence Forces. I have seen enough of war, and the death of your father and his lost honour is all that colours my mind.

"Please, I beg you to understand, and I beg you to forgive me. Please choose another life, so that never will we live with such evil again. They killed all our hope and whatever hope that may exist in my life on that night. It can never be undone, by you, or me. It was all lost. Please choose another life."

His mother cried just a little. She shed the kind of tears that just leave the eyes watery, but never fall. It was the last tear he ever saw on her face, for the remaining thirty years of her life. And it was the last time, they ever talked at length about anything. She returned to her silence and Naoyuki was left with a shell of a person, that he had only known for thirty minutes and an emptiness that no-one should ever know.

In his shock, he could think only about flowers. He sat on his small bed and drew flowers. Sometimes they were roses, sometimes cherry-blossom, sometimes tulips. He drew them for about a week, and placed them in the photo album which was now left on the small wooden table near the kitchen.

With that he was over it for a while. He enrolled in a business university. And thus he began his life again. His car crash was over. He could forget. But the sun would remain in eclipse until that day in Santa Cruz. There was only night and the moon.

A Simple Pink Shoe Box

It was so easy. He fell into a spiritual world. Better to forget all, he really wasn't anything anyway. All he was, he would never know. It was lost somewhere between the flesh and wind that flows from the morning sun. He developed no interests. His work was the same. An empty pursuit of money for nothing was his work. Being a banker meant nothing to him at all. He spent the next forty years analyzing money and approving loans. Empty nights were spent the same way, a meaningless dinner and nothings of conversations. This was the eclipse in full that he lived.

In 1964, he vowed never to have a relationship with another living thing. He could smile and live in his own thoughts and perform the endless rituals of life. A conversation with his boss and secretary was the same as breathing in and out. The bus ride home was the same. Get on the bus and sit down, watch the shadows on the street and the fog on the window during a rainy day. He was absolutely unattached to all activities. It was easy really, that's what so many of us had become. He lived without a single moment that meant anything; he could simply not see any reason for his life.

He became very successful this way. He was known as "the Buddha" at the bank and rose to prominence receiving awards from another faceless dignitary in the world. His donations to charity and temples and politicians flowed easily. His friendships were nothing, and this made for more and more friendships. He was the most popular banker ever.

Never harsh, never sharp and always agreeing were his traits and mask. No-one ever asked about his life, so all the better. They loved him more that way. The fruits of life itself fell on him, a big apartment and cars, vacations to Madagascar and Paris, the finest suits from London, and trysts with any model he wanted. It was so easy as to be ridiculous. To be absent is to be loved more. To never touch is bliss itself, and he became the master of the modern way of life.

His mother who never talked to him just smiled at all this. She grew more beautiful as she aged. He went silently with her to the sea every Sunday morning and they both threw flowers. Then he would leave and his mother would not say anything. They finally had a something, and it was nothing. Two cast-off souls, related only by their very lost situation. It was how it all should be.

He had found it so early, and though he never thanked his mother for the outburst of 1964, his life became so very comfortable because of it. When you give up, all things come. When you've nothing to push for, there is no need to push.

It was as if his mother had become a silent protector. She had in fact enveloped him in peace as she had promised his father. Her suffering and her love for his father were in fact a protection from the currents of life. He never realized this until she died.

Of course he was at her bed-side, when she closed her eyes for the last time. Of course, they never said good-bye.
He noticed something was different almost immediately. As he was leaving the hospital, a lone bird spoke from a tree. He stopped and looked up at the lone black crow. The bird called again and flew off.

It was the first time, he thought, he had ever heard a bird.

The change was stunning and became more so as he went to go and clear out her small home. We all do this. People die. We go and look at their things. We put this in a box, sit down and look at this. We think of what to keep and what to throw away.

He was doing this in his mother's bedroom when he came across a shoe-box with letters and postcards, which he had never seen. There were many letters and postcards from all over the world.

He felt like he had been hit in the head or lanced in the heart by a spear.

It was his parents' correspondence from the first letter to the last. He couldn't look at it. He quickly put the box down on the same table that the photo album was still on. He got up and looked out the window at the nearby sea. He turned back his gaze on the pink shoe-box. It held him transfixed, a simple pink shoe-box. He couldn't move for a long time, the shoe-box stood like the tallest mountain, or sky-scraper in his gaze. A simple shoe-box, lying on a small wooden table, disarmed, captured and crippled him.

He quickly left with everything in place. He didn't dare return for ten years.

Mizuko Jizo and Our Need for Love

After locking his mother's door, for some reason Naoyuki drove to Matsushima Bay, it was a short drive from their town of Shiogama, where she had lived by the sea and thrown flowers to the sea every day for fifty years. Why he went there he was not sure. He had no idea. In fact, now that she was gone he had no idea of what he was doing any more.

He parked his car by the train station and took the short walk to Oshima Island over a short bridge. He knew where he was going. Oshima was once a refuge for monks. He knew he needed to see the Mizuku Jizo which was enshrined there.

The Mizuku Jizo is a Bodhisatva who protects women and babies lost through miscarriage and abortion. All over Japan you can see the monk who holds a staff and an infant in his arm. In front of him, are little statues of infants that represent dead children lost to their parents. Sometimes there are toys or they are dressed in red bibs or clothes.

It is a very human way to mourn the loss of life that's going on every day in the world. Though we in the west abort our children now in a matter of fact way as if it means nothing, in Japan they have recognized this loss in a special and spiritual manner.

It's believed that the souls of these lost children – because they haven't lived long enough to escape the cycle of birth and rebirth – are sent to a cruel nether-world, the Hell River of Sai Na Kawara, where they struggle for redemption. In the day-time they pile rocks on the river bank hoping to be noticed by the Buddha and released from this hell and to provide themselves with refuge. At night, a demon, Shizuko No Baba, returns and destroys their shelter and beats them like a cruel step-mother. This is their eternity.

Jizo is their protector. He fears not the realms of hell and protects the children from the endless abuse of the demons in this nether-world of purgatory by the cruel and grey river of death. By offering devotion to Jizo, the parents of these lost children hope to protect them from this world of their suffering, imploring him for their eventual release. Jizo also protects travellers and expectant mothers and is especially cherished by women.

The Jizo had vowed never to leave until all evil is vanquished and all souls find themselves on the path of enlightenment. His was an ages-long sacrifice and he had vowed never to rest until all was right and suffering had ended.

Naoyuki arrived at the shrine, knelt and bowed on his knees, looking at the little statues near the Jizo. There were about one hundred little statues representing lost children. Some small toys were placed on them and he saw some flowers.

He was not sure what he was doing. Never had he cared about things like this. But today, somehow he was in the right place. Again he heard a bird singing. It was disturbing and ruined his concentration. He got up and began to walk on the path that circled the island, and he could see the pitiless ocean at his side.

The babies lost are called water-babies because they have been cruelly removed from the warmth of their mother's womb and sent to this watery grave by the river in hell. He suddenly remembered his father. He also was in a tomb in the ocean, where the "Kumano" had been sunk and destroyed. He then thought of his mother and her ashes now in the sea near her home. Water graves. Demons. Lost children. Suffering.

The ocean was a cruel place and the river of hell was full of demons.

Then mercy called him. All was not black. He knew this place was a recognition of that. The Jizo was fighting the demons, and people were calling for him to resist. The pine trees on each island in the bay were the staff of Jizo. Demons could be resisted and defeated and souls could be freed from hell.

He could see his mother and her beauty, and something drew him back to the shrine.

When he returned there was a young woman kneeling by the shrine. She was about twenty-five and crying softly in front of one of the statues. He could see the tears in her eyes as she placed a small wooden doll in front of the infant statue. The wind suddenly picked up and the trees bent with the sound of the wind.

There was something about her. He looked from a distance at her short brown hair with a strange touch of blond flowing on one side. Soon another couple came up and bowed and the young woman quickly departed; he saw her leave, the tears still on her cheek.

Mourning is a private matter. As drawn as he was to her, he dared not disturb her pain, nor disturb the couple who were also there that day to mourn another lost life. He walked around the island again.

The devotion to the Mizuko Jizo is not an ancient practice, though it is very widespread. Naoyuki knew that it was really a result of the rise of abortions in Modern Japan and destruction in the war. But at what point do we stop being infants? Surely many like his father were really children when they died in the ocean during the war. What about his father? He was in a watery grave. Surely the Jizo would have protected them too. What about their mothers? Surely they recognized that the Jizo would somehow also protect the millions lost during the war.

Lost and miscarried babies? Where does that begin and end? What about those born but lost in life? Were those, never born, somehow more equal than those who should never have been born into this world of suffering? What would the Jizo say to his mother and her fifty years of suffering? What could he say to his father? Where was the Jizo when his father was attacked by that demon, Tsuruyama? How did anything fit together in this world? He was just not sure about anything any more now that his mother was gone.

It was clear that there were demons. His mother had seen demons on that final day with his father. It was absolutely clear that he had somehow to pick sides now that his mother was gone. For the first time since 1964 he could feel something and some sort of responsibility for something more than himself and his splendid isolation. She was not there any more to protect him. It was time to be born and live for the first time. It was time to be on the side of the Jizo and fight the demons. It was time now to be born. He had to live. Now.

And there was something about that young girl. She was suffering like his mother had suffered.

He looked over at the small bridge and she was gone.

Living with Moonlight

That night was long. He left the temple and wandered aimlessly along the coast. His only companion that evening was the moon shining defiantly over the sea and land. He and the moon walked together, shoulder to shoulder. The moon was impressive beyond words, the light that pierces even the darkness. Even the clouds could not deceive it. They might overwhelm the moon for a moment as they rushed out to the ocean, but the moon refused to let them have their way for more than a minute.

Even the ocean was slave to the light of the moon. It would not allow darkness to cover up anything that night. Naoyuki thought that the moon, in her eternal defiance must be so terribly bored by the unrewarding job of lighting the world whenever the great and powerful sun is absent. Never the champion, and always the assistant, the moon had seen all things so many times. We wait for the sun to arrive and never wait for the moon. We applaud the sunrise and the fantastic sun-set. The rising moon is never the daily event. Yet that night, the moon was his champion and only solace in the new life he was living now that his mother was gone.

The hours passed as he walked with no sense of direction, his only guide being the moon that would not leave him alone to his sadness. He was neither hungry nor tired, nor was he happy. This was the first day of his life, alone. Where would he go now and what would he do with the ashes of his past life, now so decisively erased in the morning hours of his mother's death? Was he really alone with just an impartial defiant moon?

The answers were not coming to him, so he walked more. As the day began, he could see the morning dwellers driving to work, delivering newspapers, and the fisherman arguing prices at the nearby pier.

The sun was intruding now; you could see its morning light off to the distance, that time when the light changes every second and when there is a battle of light between the retreating moon and sun-rise.

This night he was living only for the moonlight and secretly hoped he could stop it disappearing for at least one day. The moon glared toward the rising sun in a distinct battle of wills. It would not give ground though you knew it would not be there for long. She was as tired as the sun was eager, but refused to leave the battlefield of night and day. Naoyuki wished the moon would hold on, but the sun was pushing her away by the minute.

Soon the light ruled and the moon was no more, Naoyuki returned to his apartment and locked the door for three weeks.

Three weeks.

For three weeks, he played the depressed role. Never shaving, never answering his phone; watching useless TV shows. Eating canned fish and crackers. It was all for no reason at all. He hardly had reason. Even he knew it was ridiculous. He was really just a child now. Stay inside, little child. Be depressed. You can. He only felt inertia, and his heart. What heart? His selfishness was beyond words. He had never felt anything for so long, he realized. The magic spell of peace and protection his mother had given him was just a form of severe laziness and his great spiritual style was just a magnificent hypocrisy. He realized he was just a fool and his mother must have known it all along, the way she smiled when he came home in his BMW on Sundays smelling of cologne, money and arrogance. He never felt anything all those years. Even her suffering was invisible to the great unfeeling one. The web of protection allowed him to transform himself into nothing. The cruelty of the truth was overpowering. Even the moon put up a better fight than he had. He was weak and uninvolved in everything and it had suited him so well and now so poorly. He had missed everything and been so content to do so. He was a cripple in every sense of the word and not good enough to inhabit even the hell of the poor children protected by the Jizo. He had nothing to mourn and no-one would mourn him. Even the lost children had more than he had.

When he realized that, he had another glass of Johnny Walker Blue. That he could afford and that would be his friend for the near future. There was no work, no friends and only Mr Johnny Walker as he mourned nothing.

Three weeks became three months and three months became a year. He did nothing for one year. Somehow his business didn't collapse, he never knew why. No-one noticed. He lived like a ghost. No-one saw anything different. No-one felt any more for him than before. Since his life was nothing, there was nothing for anyone to see differently. He was still a big boss with lots of money, only he had an unopened pink shoe-box and a locked house to go along with a locked heart.

He felt this way the day he went to have his hair cut, for no reason at all on Aoba Street. He really needed a hair-cut or so he thought. And there she was. The girl from the Jizo shrine whom he had seen the day his mother died. It was almost funny. She cut his hair and he asked her a lot of nothings. What was her name? Where did she come from? How old was she? He pretended to a big Tokyo businessman with a wife and a family.

He lied to her and asked her out to go drinking with him. He seduced her. He never mentioned that he had seen her crying in front of the Jizo. Maybe he needed someone then, and maybe he was becoming like a demon, like a Tsuruyama. It just happened that way. There was no need to over-dramatize this. Yes, he had seen her that fateful day. Now she was his lover. Maybe it was just meant to be, as if his mother had pulled them together. But maybe it was nothing. And yes, maybe he was deeply in love with her.

Her name was Chiasa. She was as simple as one could be. Her big dream was opening her own beauty salon. She had a tattoo of a rabbit on her right hand, he never asked her about it. They became a regular couple. She never asked him about his life and he was happy to listen to her stories and simple dreams. He could come and go as he pleased since he was "married with children."

The arrangement suited them both and somehow they managed very well for almost ten years. He thought about it as little as he could. Who thinks about these things anyway? When something is right we never give it a thought. We spend all of our time on disasters, and the relationships that don't work out. We think of things that aren't how they are supposed to be. We obsess on what is not what we want it to be.

Anyway, who thinks about thousands of small conversations, outings to the sea and mountains, and quiet peaceful meals together that make up something that was just meant to be?

Of course he helped her start her beauty salon and helped pay for her nearby apartment. She was grateful and loved him; that much he knew. She was a good woman. He was the problem.

But it never showed. He was the big businessman helping the hairdresser. He kept up that act and so kept his traditional distance even with his lover. But it was all par for the course. Naoyuki still had never developed the courage of the moon or of his mother or his father. He knew it too. And it made him more and more sad, every day. No-one can see nothing and that's what he had become, no matter how it pained him. The truth was both unreachable and there in front of his nose at the same time. He was like a volcano; he could hear only the rumblings. Plants grew on his sides to cover up the explosion that was only so close. But "so close" means nothing until so close arrives. So close was now so close.

The Dawn of "So Close"—My Very Own Lion-Tamer

"So close" arrived so easily and even more stupidly than his love with Chiasa. Someone had asked him to look at investing in a circus. Why, he didn't know. Again. It was just a favour for one of his "friends".

The Circus was nothing of significance. His involvement was to evaluate the investment from a purely financial perspective. Somehow he ended up being invited to the circus on a trip to Hong Kong.

Outside of the usual simple stupidity of clowns with red balloons and the thrills of gymnastics and trapeze, the main act was quite shocking. A small young man in his early twenties brought on three lions and two huge white tigers into the ring. The young man didn't weigh even half the weight of one of the white tigers. The cats were all snarling as if starved, and angry at the obvious irony of having to listen to this weak young man. They snarled more and looked fiercely around for something to attack. The young man never flinched as he made the lions roll over on their stomachs and the biggest of the tigers jump through a ring of fire. There were five fierce animals in the small ring with him and not a chance of survival if they had decided to jump him. Not a single hope of survival, the big tiger would have ripped him into three pieces in one split second. But the young man persevered through the ten minutes of humiliation that he inflicted on these regal specimens of nature. This was not a great act but it was amazing simply because the young man was so small and timid and the ferocious cats so big and fierce. Somehow he made it through the act this time.

Later that night, they went to a small coffee shop in his hotel to discuss the purchase. The lion-tamer went with them. Naoyuki learned that the lion-tamer was from Cambodia and had suffered the loss of his family during the genocide of the Khmer Rouge in the 1970s.

Naoyuki was still amazed and asked the young man, "How do you tame these animals? You're so small and they are so fierce!"

His response was crippling and his eyes glowed red when he answered. He seemed so frail and so powerful at the same time. Naoyuki thought he was speaking to a ghost or maybe a god. The great god of overcoming fear was in front him. Naoyuki listened, he died, and he changed.

"We are all so small, and life is so fierce. I simply must put away any fear, and let them know I just don't care about anything any more. They know there is no point in killing me. There is no great feast on my bones and no great victory in my destruction. Killing me would be an empty victory for them and no matter how weak I am, they obey. It is my very weakness that gives me the courage to dominate them, and their very strength which is their own defeat."

Naoyuki was stunned into silence and looked out of the window.

There, he instinctively saw a sign in Japanese lit in neon. It said simply, "Matsushima Bay".

Funny, he had stayed at this hotel before and never seen it.

He vomited instantly and excused himself saying that he was feeling very unwell.

They never bought the circus. But he had found the Matsushima Bay Restaurant and courage from his weakness.

"So close" had arrived, thanks to a slim lion-tamer.

Naoyuki Sees the Demons

The next day his first stop was the Matsushima Bay restaurant. He could not even believe it was reborn. But it was reborn. It was reborn exactly as his mother had described it. Another place maybe, another time perhaps, but the scene was exactly as his mother had described so very long ago. The painting of Mount Niitaka was there too. And yes, the food was Hiroshima style and not the Miyagi style of his Matsushima Bay.

He asked for a card, and yes, the owners were Tsuruyamas. He vomited again and rushed to his hotel with the card.

So soon had arrived. He could not believe his eyes. He could not believe his destiny. The ferocious lions were there, and yes he was as weak as a water-baby, but he had the Jizo by his side. His mother was there also.

The world had become transformed. There they were. The demons, the lions and tigers and blood on his father's face and clothes, thousands of nights of silence with a crushed mother in a crushed nation. All was there before him. This was not a transposition of time. It was the defining moment of his life. The glass prison was broken. He was really alive and like the defiant moon, could strike them down now.

Between the fear and sickness, he began to plan his revenge. It was now or never. He would not back down. No demons would push him back this time. No lies or excuses.

He rushed back to Japan and opened his mother's door and entered their home for the first time in ten years.

He froze again at the sight of the simple pink shoe-box. But he could not avoid it any more.

He read the letters for three days.

Yes, it was as he had imagined it. His parents and their world were all there in the letters, pictures and postcards. He cried at the softness, at the caring and mutual respect they had. He cried for the cruel war that separated them, and cried more when he realized that nothing could break the bond they felt.

Defeat was victory for their love. His mother's destruction and the "Kumano" set ablaze in the ocean had not destroyed anything. The demons could fail. The moon would triumph, and the Jizo would protect the small helpless children and their piles of rocks on the vicious beach. The lion-tamer in him was born. The Act was executed before a simple pink shoe-box in a dark and dusty home with the waves of the sea as witnesses. He bowed before his father and the rising moon and promised to complete his duty of vengeance against the demons, to make the lions bow and push back even the sun.

How would the Jizo push back these demons? Killing was out of the question. The Jizo would never leave until even the demons were cured. He had to push them back to give the Jizo more time to cure them of evil. There had been more than enough killing for the next ten ages.

He did some checking. Daisuke Tsuruyama had died in Hong Kong and the re-born restaurant was run by Daisuke's son Ichiru, and Daisuke's grandson Hiroshi. It was really easy to find out everything. No, they were not good men. They were really clones of Daisuke, involved in smuggling and illegal activities. There was even a picture of Ichiru and leading right-wing politicians during a visit to the Yasakuni Shrine.

He was shocked when he saw that Hirsoshi Tsuruyama was the exact clone-like replica of his grandfather, Daisuke, whom he had known from the photo album at his mother's house. The exact clone-like replica. The exact restaurant. Time had done a double flip and scored a perfect ten at the Olympics.

It was just simply a repeat of the past. The same characters doing the same things, only sixty years later. They were the ones who had destroyed Japan in the first place and now they were trying to put their tentacles back in the same places as before. They were bad men and needed to be stopped. The demons always return, which is why the Jizo is always busy. He needed to push them back, like the Jizo does every day in the River of Hell and the Desert of Punishment, to save the lost children.

Naoyuki knew how. The Jizo would guide him in this.

As his plan evolved he felt so alive. Finally he could settle scores. He hardly gave it a thought. But he knew it was going to be the final event in his life. It was his chance to push back the demons for once. He was going to make the tiger jump through the fire.

But it was more than that. He was going to end his world. He was going to lose the life he had known for so long, empty though it was. He was going to lose Chiasa and all that she meant to him. He was going to leave her and never say good-bye like he had done with his mother. How could he tell her?

He had never explained anything to anyone and now was not the time to start. There are always cracks in anything and he recognized that this was one big one. It was not the dying part of it. – The lion tamer could handle that. – It was what he had not done while he was alive and what he had not shared with anyone. But there was no getting over it. He had to revenge his mother and father and had to make something right, even if it meant that he would be no more.

He had never done anything and this was the only way out. Mistake or no mistake, there was no way out for him. The demons and lions were with him in the cage and like the skinny young man he had to push beyond himself and counter the curse that had begun with his birth. His life would mean nothing if he could not do this. Besides, he could hardly stand the person he had become.

He was ready. The rest was done the moment the bomb went off and time stopped for him.

When You Cannot See Beyond Your Own Castle

When Johnny Graham got into the Station in the morning, Naoyuki Sato was already dead, and Chief Inspector Wong was there waiting for him.

"What were you doing last night at the Matsushima Bay Restaurant? Eddie told me you had another inspection."

"Yes, Sir. That was all. The Matsushima Bay Restaurant can now be returned to the owners."

The Chief looked at him in a funny way, like he knew that Johnny was lying but not sure why.

"What's going on with this case, Graham? The Japanese Consulate-General was calling about this, and the American, Barnes is waiting for you."

"Well, here is the report so far, Chief. Make your own conclusions. It is strange and I somehow feel it will become more strange. It's your call what you want to do with this. The American might have some information, but I doubt it. They couldn't find a criminal, even if they tried, and their stock market is crashing."

"OK, Graham. I'll review this. No information to the Press."

"Yes, Sir. I wouldn't know what to say anyway."

The Chief left and Johnny Graham was left alone to his thoughts. HTK? HTK?

Philip Barnes came in, smiling.

"Good morning, Johnny."

"Good day, Philip. What are you so damn happy about? Do you have a new girlfriend or something?"

"No, not that. But yes, I do have something. We have tracked your Sato fellow to Cebu."

"Well, I told you he went to Cebu. Anything else?"

"No, we're checking in Mindanao."

"Why Mindanao?"

"That is where all the radicals are."

"Philip, you're bloody useless. You should try Santa Cruz Zambales."

"What?"

"Just forget it. If you have anything of interest let me know. I'll call you."

"Thanks, Johnny. Hope we can be friends sometime."

"Me too, Philip. Me too. Have a great day."

It was just what Johnny Graham expected. Nothing.

Next in was Tanaka, also smiling. "Hello Inspector."

"Well, Mr Tanaka, do you have any information?"

"Well, nothing new. Our Mr Sato did go to the Philippines."

"Cebu?"

"Yes, Cebu."

"That is what I told you. Do you have any more information about this crime?"

"No, not yet. We are working very hard on this. As you know, Japan is a peaceful country."

"Peaceful or not, perfect or not, Mr Tanaka, I need some information about a Japanese citizen involved in a very serious crime here in Hong Kong. I hope you can do better than that."

"We have nothing on him yet. He was a model citizen and we hope to help you and that you can keep this as quiet as possible."

"In that case, Mr Tanaka, thanks for nothing, and I'm not a model citizen. Please do get me some information that's useful."

"I will. Thank you very much."

Tanaka sped out of the room.

Eddie came in. He was looking a bit sheepish, as well he should, after telling the Chief about last night's inspection of the Matsushima Bay Restaurant. But Johnny Graham decided to keep silent. What he had done was out of the ordinary and Eddie was right to tell the Chief. Screw it anyway. Sato would probably finish the case for them before they got any information from the Americans or Japanese.

"Sir?"

"Good morning, Eddie."

"Sir, Mr John Wales from the British Consulate-General is here to see you."

"Eddie!"

"Yes, Sir."

"Tell him to piss off. ... No. Just tell him I'm too busy to see him now."

"Yes, Sir."

Johnny Graham looked at his watch. One thousand four hundred and forty minutes today. Now there were only 900 minutes left.

He called in Eddie again.

"Eddie, since this is going very slow today, are there any other major items of action today?"

"Nothing big, Sir. We will be raiding some illegal gambling sites in Tsucn Wan later tonight. Do you want to lower the staffing on this case?"

"Not sure, I'll tell you later. Thanks, Eddie."

"Thank you, Sir."

Johnny Graham went out, had a coffee and called Big Rabbit's contact. Now they were even.

When he got back to the office there were still eight hundred and twenty minutes left in the day.

He sat at his desk and thought about the case. He was busy drawing a blank for another twenty minutes. He thought about the evil Tsuruyamas for another ten minutes. He ate lunch for another twenty minutes and looked over the case some more.

Johnny Graham looked around. Yes, it was winding down. There was no new information. Soon they would be closing up the massive effort and leaving only a few detectives on it. He would move on to something else and the case would remain only partially solved. The Japanese would love it that way, and well, maybe so would everyone else. It was really like a lot of cases. Lots of smoke and no fireworks. So he reviewed everything in his mind again and again. Still nothing.

HTK.

HTK.

HTK.

At exactly 3pm when there were only five hundred and forty minutes left in the day. Eddie came in.

"Sir?"

"Yes, Eddie. Any news?"

"No, Sir. But Mr Sato's lawyer is here."

"What?"

"Mr Sato's lawyer is here."

"Say that again? I'm not hearing you."

"Mr Sato, our suspect ... his lawyer is here to see you."

Eddie looked as confused as Johnny Graham felt. Johnny didn't know what to say.

"Sir, should I tell him to come in?"

Johnny Graham didn't answer for one full minute.

"Sir?"

"Yes, Eddie. Send him in."

In walked Mr Brian Murphy, the best defence lawyer in all of Hong Kong. Johnny had known him for years and couldn't have been more surprised to see him.

Murphy could tell he was surprised.

"Why, Johnny, you look as if you've seen a ghost."

"Well, Brian, you're the last one I expected to see today."

"Well, I'm not sure what I'm doing here either. I was visited by a Mr Naoyuki Sato last week and directed to present you some documents at exactly this time. I have not read them, though I'm also charged with his defence, should a case be brought against him at a later date. He has also left some funds in my control to be given to the Hong Kong Government for unspecified damages. I'll return tomorrow at 8am after I have read his further instructions and await any charges you may bring.

"OK, Brian."

"Here are the documents. I'll see you tomorrow."

"OK, Brian. Thanks, I suppose...."

Johnny Graham opened the orange envelope and began to read.

~~~

CONFESSION AND LAST TESTAMENT OF SATO NAOYUKI

I, Sato Naoyuki, a Japanese citizen with identification number xxxxxxxx3xxx, resident of Shiogama town, Miyagi prefecture, Japan, do hereby confess to the explosion that damaged the Matsushima Bay restaurant in Causeway Bay on Nov 25th 2xxx at exactly 9.30pm. As you know there were damages and perhaps some injuries. I take full blame for this act and any charges that might result from this crime. It is my responsibility and my responsibility alone.

Samples of my fingerprints are attached and the location of the remaining bomb materials has also been attached for your final review.

The act is the direct result of damages committed by Tsuruyama Daisuke against my parents on the evening of the 7th of July 1944. The Tsuruyamas are a cruel and violent family and destroyed the honour of my father Sato Tetsu, an officer of the Imperial Japanese Navy before his final combat voyage and death on the 25th of November 1944 in the waters off Santa Cruz, Zambales, The Philippines. Please consider this as an act of revenge against this evil family with the aim of restoring my honour and the honour of my family.

I wished this to be the violence of a Japanese against Japanese, but I am also aware that there might have been injuries to innocent Hong Kong residents and I am contrite in my apology for any injuries that might have occurred. I have empowered my lawyer, Mr Brian Murphy, to bestow tomorrow a fund of three million Hong Kong dollars as restitution for any damages inflicted against innocent Hong Kong residents as a result of my action.

Why did I choose to bomb the restaurant? This is quite simple. I chose not to kill the evil Tsuruyamas, as this would have done no good. On the other hand, if I did not bomb the restaurant, the authorities in Hong Kong would have no interest in the case.

I hope that you are now getting to know the evil of the Tsuruyamas, who are involved in illegal activities and possible actions against the Chinese government on behalf of right-wing radical groups in Japan seeking to restore our destroyed empire and militaristic and violent past, which caused so much destruction throughout Asia and especially in China.

They seek to recreate a past which will lead only to more suffering in the future. Please see the attached pictures of Tsuruyama Ichiru and a Japanese former prime minister during a visit to the Yasakuni temple in Tokyo accompanied by various right-wing groups. I am sure the Chinese authorities in Hong Kong would be very offended by these acts.

Please do not take this as a complete and total renunciation of the War in the Pacific against the British, Americans and Dutch possessions. We do not apologize for a war of imperialism against imperialists. My father was proud to fight for Japan against the allies in the war. To the victor the spoils. Imperialists fighting imperialists is no different from our war against Imperial Russia in 1905.

Please remember we were your allies in World War One and it was all of you who allowed us to take the German possessions in China and turned a blind eye to our early conquests in China. Only when we attacked you in 1941, did we become the enemy. I and many Japanese believe we were forced into the war.

For our conquerors, I have no bitter feelings. Our defeat was total. You were masterful opponents in every way. Believe me, we know this. Maybe it was the wrath of God, I am not sure. You were great conquerors, you conquered us as we had never been conquered. You were not cruel. But defeat is defeat and we were defeated in every sense. Our culture was destroyed by the commercial nightmare that you called prosperity; our youth coerced by your materialism. Our territory was taken. Our military was broken. You bombed us, as if without mercy, in Hiroshima and Nagasaki and designed firebombs which slaughtered thousands upon thousands in your great fire raids in Tokyo and across the country. As you with your allies were the victors, no-one will accuse you of crimes such as these, or for your destruction of Dresden in Germany.

That is just how it is. To the victor the spoils and to the vanquished the history of the victors.

Please do not think that our defeat does not punish us, or that a single day goes by when we do not remember our defeat. We truly wanted to win. We still do, but there is no hope. All the talk about forgetting the past means nothing.

The history of nations is like the history of relationships between people. We all keep score. The British have an advantage over the Germans. The Germans have a score with the French. The Russians and Germans also have a history. The Poles have a history with the Germans and Russians. The Croats have a history with the Serbs. The French have a relationship with the Algerians. – It goes on and on. – How do our great conquerors, the Americans, feel about Vietnam, their great defeat, and the others that will come in the future? Do not think they will not come, for with total victory will also come defeat. This I promise you.

And yes, we Japanese have a relationship with our neighbours, the Koreans and the Chinese. And it is not a good one. We have never yet admitted our crimes. We were terrible to so many. We dishonoured ourselves in many places and at many times.

You will never know the pressure we feel as Japanese about this. We are pressured on the outside to admit our crimes and pressured from the inside to ignore them. Neither is acceptable. – The loss of face in admitting our errors or the lie we must live in our hearts, knowing the unspeakable crimes we have committed against the peoples of Korea and China and the other nations of Asia. – We cannot seem ever to resolve this circle. It is really an insane situation that we have.

And this is my point.

When our Prime Minister Koizumi Junichiro asked in 2001, "Why should we have to select among the dead?" in response to criticism of his visits to the Yasakuni Shrine in Tokyo, no-one answered.

I dare to answer him and all of them. I dare to answer them with my life.

Yes, we Japanese must select among the dead.

We must select from the innocents and pure on the one hand and the demons on the other hand. We must defend the innocent and pure, and push the demons away. We must in our hearts know that evil which is committed and by whom. We cannot just wash it away, because eternity is forever. We must choose between evil and good every day and in every manner possible.

My act was my way of separating the good from the evil and pushing back the demons. I had the duty to defend the honour of my father and family against the evil of the Tsuruyamas, the same militarists and demons who destroyed our country and our honour. But this is not a choice only for the Japanese, but for all nations and all people in this world. It is a choice we must make every day. We all must choose between the good and honourable and the evil every day, be they dead or alive. There is nothing else for us to do. I hope my example will somehow help stop the lies and lead us to the truth, without which there is no mercy.

My act is over.

By the time you have read this confession I will be dead. My body can be found in bungalow three of the Sand Surf and Waves Hotel in Santa Cruz, Zambales, the Philippines, where I will have had the first chance finally to say good bye to my father in his watery grave inside the battle cruiser "Kumano". Please know that he was a good and honourable naval officer and I was just doing my duty to him and my family, which will now be ended as I was an only child and have no family to continue our line.

I have suffered one thousand times and deserve to suffer many more times. I could not save my father and mother from their disgrace. I could not save my mother from fifty years of suffering. I lived a frivolous life distant from all those I should have been close to. My courage was lacking for over sixty years.

My self execution is just and I can only bow my head in shame for the great sins I have committed. I could never do enough to save those I loved, and for that failure and for my act in Hong Kong I deserve the death that has at last arrived.

Once again, I sincerely apologize to the government and people of Hong Kong for my terrible act, but I believe, if this goes to trial, which I doubt, that some will understand.

Signed Sato Naoyuki
20 November 2xxxx

~~~

Johnny Graham was speechless. He knew the case was over and that there would be no court proceedings. Sato was a genius and very, very disorientated.

Crime and Punishment? It was his job to capture the criminals so that their punishment could fit the crime. And yet, in this case, he was not sure who was more guilty – Sato or himself. Was Sato a criminal for seeking to avenge a wrong? Or was the criminal himself, Johnny, who was somehow justifying his mistake in the most trivial and selfish of ways and getting away with it. Maybe 1440 minutes would not save anything anyway and maybe Sato was right.

It was disturbing, this case. The criminal, who had committed no crime, had captured himself and the real criminals were free. Johnny Graham realized it was very hard to tell any more if it was Sato who was wrong, or the Tsuruyamas, or himself. Crime and Punishment? Maybe it was Sato who was going somehow to help all of them and yes, maybe that was his intent.

"Eddie, please get me the Chief."

"Yes, Sir."

When the Chief Inspector arrived, Johnny Graham gave him Sato Naoyuki's confession.

"Sir, here is the wrap-up on the case. I think you will be surprised and I'm glad, for once, that I'm not you. This is a tough one. I know you will know what to do. I'll wrap up the final details of the report and would like to ask for your approval for a short leave of absence."

"Graham, no problem. Where are you going on your leave?"

"I need to go to Thailand and watch some commercials. You might want to come with me, after you read this confession."

The Chief looked at him again, and this time in a very strange way. He said nothing and left the Centre with the documents.

When Brian Murphy, Sato's lawyer, came in the next day, Johnny Graham just directed him to the Chief Inspector's office. They were together for a very, very long time.

It was time to clean up shop. Like a birthday-party or a wake, the end of a case connotes a certain feeling. The excitement is gone. In this case, Sato had taken away all the excitement. They had not done anything. He had given them all the evidence. Everyone knew it too. He had taken the joy and victory from the case and left them with nothing more than a post-party mess. Well, at least he didn't do it on the cheap. He was now dead.

It was not the Americans who confirmed his death. It was the Philippine Consulate in Hong Kong. The Americans were still looking for him in Mindanao, when, as a courtesy, he called Barnes to tell him that the case was over.

The autopsy and report were very strange. But it was not the cause of death that was strange. Sato died from an overdose of sleeping pills.

Sato had arrived in Santa Cruz during the afternoon and proceeded to rent a boat to take out into Santa Cruz Bay. He had not said much. Then when the boat was in the middle of the bay, he had seen a rainbow. He asked the boatman to stop and slowly dropped a big bag of flowers into the ocean.

The sun had been setting when he returned. He then proceeded to a nearby beach and made two simple piles of rocks on the beach and sat there with the piles until the moon rose. Next to the rock piles he had written in the sand, "HTK".

Then he went back to his room and was found when the cleaning person arrived the next day.

The Philippine report was very thorough. They had interviewed all who had seen him and taken pictures. The piles of rocks and the HTK written in the sand were also photographed including several pictures of his dead body quietly lying on the bed in the hotel bungalow.

The address he had left for the bomb materials also checked out. He had apparently rented a small room in a monthly hotel, and all was there – fertiliser, bomb components and his fingerprints all over the room. There were also some pictures of the Tsuruyamas and of the Matsushima Bay restaurant. That was all.

As the Centre was being dismantled, the Chief came in only once and asked.

"Graham, this is a very strange case. You were right. Maybe I should go to Thailand with you. What does HTK mean?"

"Sir, I have no idea. I have been trying to figure it out since the first time I saw it. We may never know."

"Yes, this is very strange. Please I beg you, say nothing about the case. We are not sure what we're going to do. You realize this is very sensitive with all the comments about Japan."

"Yes, Sir, I do. I will say nothing to anyone. I know it is a tough one. I'm as confused as you."

Sato had confused the world, as if the world was not confusing enough already. He knew how confusing it was when he saw Mr Tanaka later in the day. He looked like he had seen a ghost and didn't even seem to see Johnny Graham as he walked in his running style down the hallway toward the Chief's office. He was muttering to himself. Later the Japanese Consul arrived with an even more sombre look.

Sato had confused the world. Or maybe the world had confused Sato and he was just returning the favour. Disorientation has its virtues.

Later in the day, an envelope arrived. Inside were air tickets and hotel vouchers for a two-week vacation to Phuket, Thailand. The envelope was white and not bright orange. For this Johnny Graham was relieved. On the envelope was a picture of a rabbit.

Yes. The Big Rabbit was master of all. Helping someone means helping someone again. All was tranquil again. Hong Kong would go on. He would, too, he hoped.

High Tide: Sculpted Sand and Two Piles of Rocks

Johnny Graham had a nice but disturbing trip. The beach was beautiful, the sand soft and the women kind. He would get drunk every night, sleep all day and then go out for more.

Then he had a relapse. He felt disturbed by everything and the vacation was turning sour. He cured this by piling up two piles of rocks to defy the sea everyday. This was something he could do for his departed wife and small daughter. He was just struggling again, just like before. He, however, didn't write, "HTK", since he had never figured out what Sato meant by this.

This activity and watching commercials finally calmed him down. He might be able to get back to the old Johnny Graham that had been so confused by Sato. Ever since he had read Sato's confession, the one thousand four hundred and forty minutes had not been working. Johnny had to get back to where he had been. He was not sure, however, if he could. He was guilty. Sato was not. The Tsuruyamas were guilty too. He hoped they would get punished also.

Johnny Graham knew, once again, that his punishment could never be enough.

He was suddenly convinced that nothing was random. Sato has disproved his theory, and maybe all of his theories. He would just have to go back to the drawing-board. He would just have to figure out something new. But piling up rocks on the beach seemed like a good idea. He was not sure what Sato meant by this but it just felt right.

When Johnny arrived back in Hong Kong, it was like a dream.

There had been many changes. People were different. It was all like a strange dream.

It was like leaving a town and climbing up a mountain, and when you come back down every one is gone. The world that you knew has vanished and you have that last man on earth feeling. As much as you hated being with them all, you missed them when they were gone. The last man on earth.

The Chief had put in his resignation. Then he had taken it back. And then he was promoted to another position in the Government. He did stop in to say goodbye to Graham but never brought up the case again. They would always remain friends.

Eddie Lo was deservedly promoted and moved to another Division. He stopped in to say goodbye and also never said one word about the Sato case or any case that they had worked on. Johnny saw him from time to time after that, but the relationship had changed. Eddie was now an Inspector and there were no more, "Yes, Sirs" out of his mouth. He was still the best and always would be. Johnny Graham could not count how many heroes he had met in the Hong Kong Police Force, but Eddie Lo was one of the finest.

Philip Barnes, the American, was removed from his position after falling in love with a Philippina from Mindanao whom he had met in a bar in Wanchai. He apparently lost his security clearance and was sent back to the States. His replacement was even more distant, but the American retreat with honour from Iraq and the collapse of the world economy was making everyone even more distant. Johnny Graham was sorry that he had always been so rough on him. Everyone deserves a chance at love. He was glad that Philip Barnes was taking his chance. In his heart he wished him well.

John Wales from the British Consulate-General became involved in an investment scandal in the United Kingdom and was sent back home. He didn't say goodbye. Johnny Graham never found out if he was convicted for financial crimes. Probably not. Bankers never lose, and he could not say he was sorry to see him go.

Mr Tanaka was quickly replaced and sent back to Japan.

Colonel Chan and Major Wu didn't come back. Johnny Graham guessed they didn't need to. Victory is sweet and revenge even sweeter. He was not sure that he had even met them. His meetings with Major Wu were just a lost memory now.

Funny, how we cannot seem to hold onto anything in this world. Memories are not real. They are just something that helps us disorient ourselves from the current moment, which is all we have and all we ever had. But then, he suddenly remembered that his won-ton soup that night with Major Wu was excellent.

It just goes on and on.

The case against Mr Sato was never tried in a public court, nor mentioned again. It was as if it had never happened.

Looking back, Johnny Graham was not sure if he had even known about it. He never asked what happened to the money Sato had left.

In the end, the case had never happened, at least publicly. And the funny thing was, that, even though it never happened, it was destined to affect his life greatly. It was a mystery that no-one would ever discuss again. Mr Sato had changed him so very much. But he too, like the case, had never existed.

Well, at least he had Big Rabbit, and always would. ... Hong Kong boys forever!

A Raindrop as it Strikes the Dust

The day that Johnny Graham went on vacation to Thailand, a package wrapped in orange arrived for Chiasa. Inside were two bright orange envelopes and a simple pink shoebox and an old photo album.

One envelope said, "Chiasa, please open this envelope first."

Chiasa opened the envelope and read the enclosed letter.

Dearest Chiasa,
I am very sorry for not contacting you. A lot has happened. Please sit down, and open the next envelope. Dearest, Please read the letter. I hope you will understand.
Naoyuki.

Chiasa sat down and opened the second envelope and began to read the second letter.

Dearest Chiasa,
I am not even sure how to begin this. This will all come as a great shock to you. In fact this is the hardest letter I have ever had to write to you. But it is necessary.
We all lose those we love in life. I have lost both my parents and so much that I cherish. The hardest loss of my life will be you.
I am not sure even what to say. Just understand that what has happened has nothing to do with you or us, or our love.
I have committed a very serious crime and will not be returning to you as I left you. It is all very complicated and I do not want you even to try to understand it. The sad fact is that for me, life is over.
First of all, let me tell you the truth.
I was not married, even though I told you I was. Sadly, though you were the most important person in my life, I lacked

the courage to tell you the truth. This is my great mistake. I should have confided my innermost thoughts and never did.

I have never been married, and you were the only real relationship I had in my life. Yes, financially I was very successful. That is the truth.

Except for the time with you and several meaningless relationships, I lived in Shiogama, very near to my mother, who died about the time I met you. I really wished that she had known you. You would have made her very happy.

I am sorry that I have been so untruthful to you. I hope you will forgive me and understand. It is just that I could never bring myself to get close to anyone in this life. This was my error.

My actions were artificial and untrue. I was never able, until recently, even to summon the most basic courage. I am so sorry and apologize for the weakness I have shown in this life.

I saw you the first time, not in the beauty shop, but at the Mizuko Jizo Shrine in Matsushima Bay. Do you remember the day? You were there and crying. That was also the day that my mother died and my life changed. Before you she was my Protector, My Goddess and My Only Love.

I have always believed that it was my mother who led me to see you on that sad day for both of us. I know you were suffering for something, and I should have tried to get to know you and learn of your pain, but I never did. I hope you can forgive me.

Now that I am soon to leave this world, I suddenly can feel, and I know that you were suffering.

But do know that I tried to help you in every way I could, as you helped me by being the only true love of my life.

I am sorry that I was not honest and we were never married, and that we never had children and a family. Perhaps our ages were too far apart. Perhaps it was destiny. I am sorry.

Chiasa, you and I both know that we had a wonderful love. The feeling we had together was always just right. When you meet the love of your life, you know. When the feeling is right, you know. Ours was a deep and pleasant love.

I knew this with you, and you knew this with me.

When you're lucky enough to experience this one great love, it is special. For my life, that love was you.

My greatest error was not telling you this when we were together. My greatest error was not recognizing the good in life until too late. My greatest error was not understanding that one day all will end, and we must live as if there was no tomorrow and not be afraid of embracing life and love as it is there for us every moment.

I deeply regret that it took me so long to see and understand. We treat our lives as such a routine. One day runs into the next and we never stop to see the wonder.

Chiasa, you were my wonder. You were my miracle. You were my saviour and the protector of my heart.

As I told you, I cannot go into why I did what I did. The simple pink shoe-box has letters from my parents and postcards from during the war.

Please read them.

My parents had a perfect love as you will see and I deeply regret I could not replicate their love exactly with you.

In the pink shoe-box, there are also keys to a house and the address is in the box. The home is now yours as you were my only family member. Also, please know that your beauty salon has been paid for in full and there is an extra amount of money which I hope will provide for you as you age.

My parents could not say good-bye to each other. An unfortunate incident and the war ended their chance for a life.

My father died during the war in the Pacific in the Philippines aboard the Cruiser "Kumano", where he still rests in a watery grave. I never knew him as I was born after he died. I have gone finally to say good-bye to him.

I never said good-bye to my mother. I had the chance, but I did not take it. Not saying good-bye to her after she had suffered so much was another of my great mistakes.

Chiasa, everything in life ends. Why do we find it so hard to say good-bye?

Those we love pass away, or we leave them and we never say goodbye. We are always searching for more and forgetting what is in front of us. I lived a life where I never saw the clearest things and was blind to everything.

When I saw you at the temple I knew that you were crying for a lost child. I knew that you were trying to protect your water-baby from the ravages of the demons in the River of Hell. The Jizo has heard your prayers and I am sure that he will defend your child and bring peace.

Chiasa, I could not leave this earth without saying good-bye to you. I failed to say good-bye to my mother and I failed to appreciate the life that I had and those around me. Now I must finally find the courage to say good-bye.

I beg you to have a happy life when I am gone. I wish you peace and happiness and thank you for the love and all that you gave me. Please do remember me and my parents. You're the only one who is left to take care of our memory. May the Jizo protect us all!

Please do not cry too much. This world has already had more than it needs of suffering. Please try to understand.

I love you forever, though I may not be here with you.

Good-bye My Dearest.

Your Love, Naoyuki

Chiasa read the letter once more; then passed the night crying loudly.

Later, she did read the letters and postcards in the simple pink shoe-box. Over time she came to understand just a little of what Naoyuki said and what he meant. As she aged, his words and tenderness became clear and she knew what she must do as his wife in his eternal absence.

Postscript I

Johnny Graham continued on. Johnny Graham struggled on. Sato had changed him and he never knew why. He continued solving cases and studying disorientation. It was really his life's work. He could never shake off what he had done. He could never shake off his own dishonour. He was always going to be a broken man.

But somehow, he felt better. And he would keep trying to work through this. Randomness just simply does not exist. When he had found the right pieces, the puzzle would be complete. Scar or no scar, he was just going to climb the mountain of life.

Thank God for the Hong Kong Police and the mercy of Chief Inspector Wong. They had saved him as they save everyone, which is why Hong Kong is and always will be one of the world's safest cities. He was glad that he would always be a member of the Hong Kong Police.

Several months after Sato died, Johnny Graham received a package addressed from China. In it was a letter from Major Wu and a small picture of Chairman Mao.

He read the letter.

Dear Inspector Graham,
  Best Greetings from China.
  I think this time we got your address right after we failed with your license plate before? Yes? We are trying to do a better job every day.
  Just a short note to wish you a Happy and Prosperous Chinese New Year. I have been transferred to Wuhan in Hubei. I never took the time to thank you for your help, but please know that I will always be your friend. China is still a poor country and we have suffered a lot. We have had a hard road to development and a very long history.

I am glad that you have been such a good friend of China. Thank you for your help.

If you are ever in Hubei, you always have a home with me.

Anyway, remember Chairman Mao is always smiling. I wish the same for you.

Until we meet again.

Mr Wu.

Well, that was something. Major Wu was really a good guy after all.

Several weeks later the news came out of the Chinese news services. A large and complicated Japanese spy-ring had been broken in Qingdao and Dalian. Several dozen Japanese Spies and Front Companies had been dismantled. There had been quite a few arrests. It was a major incident.

A few weeks later, Japan and China signed a formal agreement on sharing oil exploration rights off the Senkaku/Diaoyutai Islands. The agreement was largely in line with the earlier Chinese demands and represented an abrupt turn around for the Japanese on this issue.

In addition, the new Japanese Prime Minister had vowed not to visit the Yasakuni Shrine during his term in office so as to avoid insult to other nations in Asia.

The Matsushima Bay Restaurant was never reopened. He passed by the spot once and in its place was a foreign fast-food chain.

He never heard of the Tsuruyamas again and never asked. The Sato case had simply never happened. The demons were gone from Sato's life and, come to think of it, Graham was feeling very demon-free himself. He wished he could thank Mr Sato.

He did keep the picture of the two piles of stones with "HTK" written in the sand. He kept it at home above his TV set so that he could look at it, when he wasn't watching the commercials.

He never figured out what "HTK" meant. Maybe he never would. Maybe it was not that important.

PostScript 2

Naoyuki Sato and Chiasa Honda's son, Tetsu Sato, was born later that year.

Chiasa is raising him in peace and they have become very good friends. Tetsu is a very bright boy and loves to look at his father's photo album and read the letters of love of his grandparents. He tries to draw flowers like his father once did. Also, he's learning English, as his father and grandfather did. He has a very warm heart and promises always to take good care of his mother.

Every Sunday, Chiasa and young Tetsu go to the sea and throw flowers to remember his father and his grandparents. Sometimes they go to visit the Mizuko Jizo in Matsushima Bay and ask for his help, so that all souls and those suffering will one day be brought to enlightenment.

The End

Acknowledgements

For acting as Consultant on Police Procedure: Mr Tony Carroll.

Permission was kindly given by Bob Hackett for verbatim quotations from "HIJMS KUMANO: Tabular Record of Movement", © 1997-2008 Bob Hackett and Sander Kingsepp. Revision 5, found at the following website: http://www.combinedfleet.com/kumano_t.htm

Information about the final resting place of the "Kumano" was obtained from Tony Tully's, "Located / Surveyed Shipwrecks of the Imperial Japanese Navy".

The front cover illustration is based on a copyright photo by Mark Schumacher, "http://www.onmarkproductions.com/jizo-six-hase-dera-kamakura.JPG", found at "www.onmarkproductions.com/html/jizo1.shtml#six".

The back cover photograph of Cruiser *Kumano*, is from A503 FM30-50 booklet for identification of ships, published by the Division of Naval Intelligence of the Navy Department of the United States and is believed to be in the public domain.

Please let the publishers know if any oversight has occurred. We will include any needed additional acknowledgement in the next practicable publication of this title.

WINNERS OF THE PROVERSE PRIZE 2009-2016
Rebecca Tomasis, for her novel, "Mishpacha – Family"
Laura Solomon, for her young adult novella, "Instant Messages"
Gillian Jones, for her novel, "A Misted Mirror"
David Diskin, for his novel, "The Village in the Mountains"
Peter Gregoire, for his novel, "Article 109"
Sophronia Liu, for her collection of sketches, "A Shimmering Sea"
Birgit Linder, for her illustrated poetry collection, "Shadows in Deferment"
James McCarthy, for his biography, "The Diplomat of Kashgar"
Philip Chatting, for "The Snow Bridge and Other Stories"
Celia Claase, for her essay and poetry collection, "The Layers Between"
Lawrence Gray, for his novel, "Adam's Franchise"
Gustav Preller, for his novel, "Curveball: Life never comes at you straight"
Ivy Ngeow, for her novel, "Cry of the Flying Rhino".

WINNERS OF SUPPLEMENTARY PRIZES 2009-2016
Victor E. Apps, for his young adult novella, "The Perilous Passage of
Princess Petunia Peasant"
Rupert Kwan Yun Chan, for his autobiography, "Chocolate's Brown Study
in the Bag"
Sally Dellow, for her poetry collection, "Wonder, Lust & Itchy Feet"
Patricia Glinton-Meicholas, for her poetry collection, "Chasing Light"
Lawrence Gray, for his collection of short stories, "Odds and Sods"
Patricia W. Grey, for her novel, "Death has a Thousand Doors"
Emily Ho, for her "Memoirs of an Ice-Cream Lady"
Henrik Hoeg, for his poetry collection, "Irreverent Poems for Pretentious
People"
L.W. Illsley, for his young adult epic poem, "Astra and Sebastian"
Akin Jeje, for "Smoked Pearl: Poems of Hong Kong and Beyond"
Lelawattee Manoo-Rahming, for "Immortelle and Bhandaaraa Poems"
James Norcliffe, for his poetry collection, "Shadow Play"
Jan Pearson, for her novel, "Red Bird Summer"
Jan Pearson, for her novel, "Tiger Autumn"
Jan Pearson, for her novel, "Black Tortoise Winter"
Jason S Polley, for his poetry collection, "refrain"
Jason S Polley, for "cemetery miss you"
Shahilla Shariff, for her poetry collection, "Life-Lines"
Hayley Ann Solomon, for her poetry collection, "Celestial Promise"
Laura Solomon, for her young adult novella, "University Days"
Laura Solomon, for her novel, "Hilary and David"
James Tam, for his novel, "Man's Last Song"
Dennis Wong, for his novel, "Revenge From Beyond"

131

CHINA, HONG KONG & South-East ASIA FICTION
PUBLISHED BY PROVERSE

Andy Carter. Bright Lights and White Nights. 2015.

Peter Gregoire. Article 109. 2012.
(Winner of the Proverse Prize 2011.)

Peter Gregoire. The Devil You Know. 2014.

Lawrence Gray. Cop Show Heaven. 2015.

Dragoş Ilca. HK Hollow. 2017.

Caleb Kavon. The Monkey in Me. 2009.

Caleb Kavon. The Reluctant Terrorist.2011.

Caleb Kavon. Paranoia. 2012.

Ivy Ngeow. Cry of the Flying Rhino. 2017.
(Winner of the Proverse Prize 2016.)

Jan Pearson. Black Tortoise Winter. 2016.

Jan Pearson. Red Bird Summer. 2014.

Jan Pearson. Tiger Autumn. 2015.

Jason S Polley. Cemetery Miss You. 2011.

James Tam. Man's Last Song. 2013.

Paul Ting. Bao Bao's Odyssey: From Mao's Shanghai to Capitalist Hong Kong.

CHINA, HONG KONG & MACAU NON-FICTION PUBLISHED BY PROVERSE

Jean A. Berlie. The Chinese of Macau: A Decade after the Handover. 2012.

Gillian Bickley, Ed. The Complete Court Cases of Magistrate Frederick Stewart. 2008.

Gillian Bickley. Ed. The Development of Education in Hong Kong, 1841-1898 as Revealed by the Early Education Reports of the Hong Kong Government 1848-1896. 2002.

Gillian Bickley. The Golden Needle: The Biography of Frederick Stewart (1836-1889). 1997.

Gillian Bickley, Verner Bickley, Christopher Coghlan, Timothy Hamlett, Geoffrey Roper, Gary Tallentire. Ed Gillian Bickley. A Magistrate's Court in Nineteenth Century Hong Kong. 1st ed. 2005, 2nd ed. 2009.

Rupert Chan. Chocolate's Brown Study in the Bag. 2011.

Major (Ret'd) Brian Finch, MCIL. A Faithful Record of the Lisbon Maru Incident. 2017. Translation from Chinese with additional material. 2017.

George Washington (Farley) Heard. Through American Eyes: The Journals (18 May 1859 - 1 September 1860) Of George Washington (Farley) Heard (1837-1875). Edited by Gillian Bickley. 2017.

Emily Ho. Memoirs of an Ice-Cream Lady. 2011.

Sophronia Liu. A Shimmering Sea: Hong Kong Stories (Winner of the Proverse Prize 2012). 2013.

James McCarthy. The Diplomat of Kashgar: A Very Special Agent. The Life of Sir George Macartney, 18 January 1867 to 19 May 1945. (Winner of the Proverse Prize 2013). 2014.

Stuart McDouall. All Agog In China. 2014.

Lt. Cmdr. Henry C.S. Collingwood-Selby, R.N. (1898-1992). Richard Collingwood-Selby (Chile) and Gillian Bickley (Hong Kong), Eds. In Time of War. 2013.

FIND OUT MORE ABOUT PROVERSE AUTHORS, TITLES, EVENTS AND LITERARY PRIZES

Visit our website: http://www.proversepublishing.com
Visit our distributor's website: <www.chineseupress.com>

Follow us on Twitter
Follow news and conversation: twitter.com/Proversebooks>
OR
Copy and paste the following to your browser window and follow
the instructions: https://twitter.com/#!/ProverseBooks

"Like" us on www.facebook.com/ProversePress

Request our free E-Newsletter
Send your request to info@proversepublishing.com.

Availability
Most titles are available in Hong Kong and world-wide
from our Hong Kong based Distributor,
The Chinese University of Hong Kong Press,
The Chinese University of Hong Kong,
Shatin, NT, Hong Kong SAR, China.
Email: cup-bus@cuhk.edu.hk. W: <www.chineseupress.com>.

All titles are available from Proverse Hong Kong,
http://www.proversepublishing.com

Ebooks
Many of our titles are available also as Ebooks.

www.ingramcontent.com/pod-product-compliance
Lightning Source LLC
Chambersburg PA
CBHW051346020726
47501CB00007B/2297